FAR FROM HEAVEN

HEAVEN

Christopher C. Moore

PublishAmerica
Baltimore

Hardcover 978-1-4560-3622-5
Softcover 978-1-4560-3621-8
PUBLISHED BY PUBLISHAMERICA, LLLP
www.publishamerica.com
Baltimore

Printed in the United States of America

To my family,
for believing in me.

"Desperation is the raw material of drastic change. Only those who can leave behind everything they have ever believed in can hope to escape."
~William S. Burroughs

BIG TIME PLAYER

Ol' Jim sat on his stool backstage and let the melodies of the opening band wrap around his body like a warm blanket as he swayed gently from side to side. *Long Gone Apparition* they called themselves: Four yuppie punks straight out of college, but Ol' Jim liked the way the cats grooved. They're a more known act but were going on first because Ol' Jim always headlined at The Warhorse; it was his place to play and these were his people. Everybody sure loved Ol' Jim.

The guitar case laid flat on its back on the floor in front of the stool, glimmering black in the dim light coming from the front of the bar. Ol' Jim bent down slowly, being mindful of his back, and ran his fingers gingerly along the edges of the case until he found the brass lock hinges. He lingered there a second, straining his eyes to read the white letters inscribed against the blackness of the case.

James Edward Reeves, Jr.

"The Scavengers"

Ol' Jim released the brass hinges and lifted the lid slowly, as he always does, reached down and carefully brought out the guitar as if he were holding a child. The one and only treasure in his life, this old guitar: Shaped and carved from mahogany, the base painted in a dark maroon fading into a seductive red, the neck a dark brown and the whole thing shined to perfection. *Ruby*, that's what he called her. Ol' Jim had known that was her name the second he had laid his eyes on her in the spring of

'61. He and Ruby bad been through a lot together and, after all of the heartache and despair, they still kept going.

"We make quite the team, don't we baby?" He whispered to Ruby, bending down to kiss her glossy finish.

Sitting up straight, with Ruby on his lap, Ol' Jim began to hum to himself quietly. He softly plucked one chord after the other, feeling the vibrations and listening to the sweet sounds. With Ruby in tune and resting in his lap, Ol' Jim closed his eyes and tapped his foot against the stool as the guys were wrapping up their set. His fingers shook slightly but he steadied them quickly, the anticipation was building in Ol' Jim. Tonight was going to be his best show ever, the one he was remembered for. After tonight, after all these years, Ol' Jim was finally going to make it to the big time.

On stage, the final chords of the song sounded and a "thank you" was mumbled into the microphone which was followed by an enthusiastic round of applause. Ol' Jim stood and listened to the people cheer and clap, basking in its essence as if it were for him. It would be, soon enough. The band walked back stage talking amongst themselves, laughing and smiling apparently happy with their performance. They didn't even notice Ol' Jim standing just a few feet from them in the midst of the shadows. He hoped they would stay to hear his songs.

"Ladies and gentlemen," Donny, the bartender and resident MC, said as the crowd was dying down, "you know him, you love him—give it up for Ol' Jim."

An intermittence of applause filled the air as Ol' Jim stepped out onto the stage, lugging the stool behind him. There were a lot of faces in the crowd that he didn't recognize, most likely ones who came to see the other band. They all looked at him solemnly, expecting to be entertained. Well, Ol' Jim would oblige—they would all bear witness to his legend. He placed the stool in front of the microphone.

"Thanks, Donny," he muttered and then lowered the microphone as he sat on the stool and put Ruby into position. Silence radiated off the walls as everyone waited for him to begin. "A one, a two, a one two three…"

Ruby's music filled the air as he plucked each string methodically, applying the right amount of pressure and timing to each note.

> *Time, the time it is rolling*
> *Far, far past, where it should be*
> *God can't make it stop for nothin'*
> *Not even for you and me*
> *Yes, it's leavin' us behind*

Ol' Jim tapped his foot on the floor as some of the crowd began to clap along with the rhythm. The song had an old sound to it because he had written it as a young man. It was Ol' Jim's Nana that had taught him to play, at the ripe age of twelve. It was strange for a woman to play guitar back then, especially using the lower, darker sounding chords. Many people didn't approve, but Ol' was fascinated with the music she created, intoxicated by the slow, thunderous melodies. Ol' Jim had written this particular song when he was seventeen. After he had finished playing to his Nana for the first time, she looked him dead in the eyes and said, "Son, you're gonna be a big time player. Yes you are," and took another drag from her cigarette.

When he was done with the song the people applauded loud and long. Everybody sure loved Ol' Jim.

"Thank you," he said as everyone quieted down. "That was a song near and dear to my heart called *Losing Time*." He straightened the microphone a bit. "I'm Ol' Jim Reeves and thank y'all for comin' out tonight. And how about them other boys?" Another roaring applause scrambled through the room as the guys from *Long Gone Apparition* waved to everyone from the side of the stage. Ol' Jim waited for everyone to simmer down again. "Now, this is an old song: A hit from way back in the summer of '71, called *You Wouldn't Believe.*"

A whoop was let out into the air. Ol' Jim didn't even have to look up to know that it was Daniel Teague who had let it out. Daniel was probably the only one besides himself that remembered the glory of the song, how it had propelled *The Scavengers* almost to stardom. Almost.

Ol' Jim began tapping out a slow beat against Ruby's glossy finish and after several seconds the crowd caught on and followed suit.

I know you're troubles come unseen
But that don't mean you can't get past the past

He stops tapping out the beat and lets silence fill the air for a second, but only for a second. "A one, two, three," and the chords that follow produce a melody that Ol' Jim has heard hundreds of thousands of times, but every time he plays it he plays it like it's the first time.

We know only what we know
And nothing else
But that don't mean
There isn't help to be found when you're low
So low there ain't no high

There is a pause of words as Ol' Jim's fingers cross the strings and the song from his soul cries out to the ears of anyone who will listen.

You wouldn't believe what I've been through
The cold, the desert, the mountains, the depths
I've climbed back from hell itself
You wouldn't believe what I've been through
Just to get back to you

•

You Wouldn't Believe was the first and only hit for *The Scavengers* in the summer of 1971. Ol' Jim had formed the band back in '67 with his long time friend Tony Richmond—Ol' Jim did the playing and Tony did the singing. Tony, or simply "T" as he preferred, had a soprano voice with power and movement in the most subtle of ways. At first when you heard him, you didn't quite know what was happening but soon it became clear that you were under his spell as he bellowed verse after verse. It had always been magical to Ol' Jim.

Starting off as just a guitar and a voice, they quickly gained a small local following. It stayed this way for three years—playing local gigs, making a few bucks and gaining very little recognition—and Ol' Jim just couldn't figure why they weren't going anywhere.

"*We ain't got no rhythm, man,*" *T said, drumming an unopened pack of cigarettes against his palm.*

Ol' Jim couldn't do nothin' but shake his head. "*Nah, that ain't right. We got rhythm, don't we baby,*" *he said to Ruby and strummed a few chords in quick succession,* "*in spades.*"

"*But people want the power, the boom, the bass; we need to step it up a notch or two.*" *T removed a cigarette and lit it with his zippo.* "*I know this guy who plays drums like a demon's grabbed hold of his hands,*" *he said through a cloud of smoke.*

Ol' Jim hung his head and strummed out a quick, lonely tune. "*Fine.*"

His Nana had told Ol' Jim that that guitar of his was all he would ever need to make it. And, even though he played Ruby like hell, he thought maybe T was right—maybe all they needed was to liven up their sound.

T introduced Ol' Jim to Marcus Waters, a machinist from a local factory who spent the majority of his free time drinking and banging away on his drums. Ol' Jim was still hesitant, but after he heard Marcus play, he knew the addition would be a perfect match. With Marcus now in the crew, the three set out to find a bassist. They put up fliers and ads in the newspaper, with little to no results, in the weeks that followed. A few guys auditioned for them, and they were all talented, but Ol' Jim could hear as soon as they started playing that it wasn't what they needed. Then, on a breezy September afternoon, Jackson Thompson strolled up, plugged in and set to playing a tune that lit Ol' Jim on fire. He watched Jackson's fingers dance over the neck and as he hit each chord it felt like lightning striking the earth. Ol' Jim shook the man's hand and that was it—*The Scavengers* were complete.

T wrote most of the words, creating the feel while Ol' Jim laid down the tune and the timing, Jackson and Marcus followed his path adding their own signature sounds into the melodies. They practiced whenever there was time and always with feverish determination. Within several months, the band had eleven solid songs and began to play gigs. It was February, 1971 and Ol' Jim knew that they were all gonna be big time players.

In no time it was April and Ol' Jim had never been happier—*The Scavengers* were playing to packed bars and clubs all around the county—and several surrounding cities—a couple of nights a week. Their name was getting out there and real money was starting to come in. Best of all for Ol' Jim, a lot of the time when he would go somewhere, someone would come up to him and say, "*Hey, you're the guitarist in that band.*"

"*Yes,*" he would say with a big grin on his face, "*yes, I am.*"

One early morning in mid-April, Ol' Jim woke from a fitful sleep—the last traces of a terrifying dream lingering still in his memory and the words to the band's soon-to-be hit song on his tongue. He worked fervently with Ruby all of that day and half way into the next trying to get the music just right; that perfect balance between heaven and hell. When, at least, he thought he had obtained that perfection, Ol' Jim called T over to his trailer and laid the song down for him.

"*That was...that was the most wonderful thing I've ever heard,*" *T stammered out when he had finished playing the song. Ol' Jim just smiled as he looked at T's eyes wide in disbelief. T lit a cigarette and exhaled slowly, giving an incredulous sigh. He coughed slightly and then, recovering himself, asked, "What do you call it?*"

"*You Wouldn't Believe,*" *Ol' Jim said, holding Ruby tight, "that's what I dreamt its name would be.*"

The guys worked on the song for a couple of weeks and then officially added it to their set list. It was an instant hit with everyone. Every time they played, when they were done, the crowd would sit in silence for a several seconds as if thoroughly contemplating what they had just heard and then applauded enthusiastically. Ol' Jim would always nod and smile, all the while politely saying "thank you," feeling as if he were on top of the world.

In early June, *The Scavengers* finally cut a record featuring *You Wouldn't Believe* on Side A and a song T had written called *On The Wind* on Side B. Ol' Jim thought T would be upset about his song being on the back side because he was the actual song writer of the band. But, as it turns out, T—like everybody else—was just happy as hell to be recording a record. T gave the record to a friend of his who was a local DJ and within no time *You Wouldn't Believe* was being played on the radio, a lot.

A few weeks after the song was broadcasted, *The Scavengers* were approached by an agent from a fast rising new label that was getting bigger by the minute. The man wore a suit that glistened when the light hit it and an expensive pair of shades that held their reflections. He told them that if they signed with his label not only would they continue making records and getting air play but they would also tour venues across the mid-west, for starters. And, oh yeah, they would make lots and lots of money. The man smiled the kind of smile that should be reserved for the devil himself. The guys took a minute to deliberate and then all shook the man's hand and went inside to sign the papers.

It was a month into the tour and everyone was feeling invincible—*You Wouldn't Believe* was getting enough air time so that they heard it at least once a day and everywhere they went they were playing to packed crowds. Ol' Jim knew that this was it; they were going to the big time. That was, until one night at a bar in Cleveland. The night had been going well. The place was crowded as usual and the electricity from the patrons was flowing as they sang and screamed and jumped around. T was in the middle of singing when he was seized by a raging coughing fit. After half a minute when he didn't recover the guys stopped playing to see if he was okay. T went down to one knee, vomited up blood and then passed out at the sight of it.

Everybody knew what was wrong with T before he even saw the doctor: Lung cancer, and pretty advanced by the time they took the x-rays. After fifteen years of smoking two packs a day the doctors didn't know how he had been able to sing for so long, they also didn't give him much longer to be walking around. Ol' Jim and the guys wanted to stick around and comfort T, they were all like family now, but they also had obligations that had to be filled. The label said that *The Scavengers* had to find a new singer and get back on the road. Auditions were held and lots of people came but no one was a good fit. Finally, Marcus and Jackson convinced Ol' Jim to do it. Everyone knew that he could sing, he was just a little shy about it.

So they set out again to finish the tour with Ol' Jim in front of the microphone. But, even though he sang well, it soon became apparent that his low and gruff voice didn't go with the songs that the band had written—the guys knew it and so did the fans. No one could replace T and *The Scavengers* were dead in the water as one hit wonders. The label ripped up the contract and sent them packing, back home to their former lives where things would never be the same.

•

Ol' Jim finished singing, played the last few notes and then let Ruby rest. The patrons of The Warhorse sat in silence for a second as if unaware of what to do, but then applause erupted. A smile crossed Ol' Jim's face. It wasn't as perfect as it had once been with T belting out the words and the guys playing with him, but it was still his song and it was still a crowd pleaser.

"Thank you," he said grabbing the mike, "once again, that was *You Wouldn't Believe.* Now, I'm gonna change up the pace a little and play you a slower song called *Underneath the Night.* I wrote this a long time ago for someone very special."

An expecting hush fell over the room as everyone waited for the next song to start. Ol' Jim set out with a slow, dark, and pleasing riff. Ruby's strings quivered under his fingertips as he plucked each note with finite precision.

> *Now that we've seen all that can be*
> *Why won't our eyes close and sleep*
> *The dreams wait for the time*
> *When they can be free among the dead*
> *But they can't uncross that line*
> *And we'll never live down this dread*

Ol' Jim looked up as he continued playing to see their faces—some people just stared straight ahead but many had their eyes closed and were swaying along with the haunting rhythm that he created. He played faster for a few seconds as the chorus approached, looking for that perfect sound.

> *Why can't we be left alone*
> *The evil and the fear in their eyes*
> *They say you're a witch in the darkness*
> *But I know that underneath the night*
> *You're home*

•

This song was great because it had the benefit of being true. His Nana had been a witch. Well, according to everyone in the town where Ol' Jim had grown up, anyway. Any woman who had two children and no husband, and who sat out on her porch drinking and playing "the devil's music" with a guitar, couldn't be anything other than a witch. Ol' Jim's mother and uncle's lives hadn't been easy, and neither had his by extension. Any misfortune or troubles felt by anyone in the town was blamed on the Baine family—his Nana's name. Martha Baine's children, and her only grandchild, were tormented by their peers and ridiculed as second-class outsiders by everyone.

This was only hearsay, of course; speculation, whispers through the town's ears. What no one could know, what no one could understand, is that they were right. Martha Baine practiced the secrets of the unseen forces that everyone called "witch craft." She cursed those who crossed her and cast "spells" for her own amusement. Although, the Baine family had seen its share of curses and hardships as well: Martha had been an only child and orphaned at a young age, moreover the only two men she had taken as lovers in her life both died in equally horrible and tragic accidents. But she did have her children from the experiences—her boy, Zane, who died at the age of twenty-three by drowning in a lake, and Anna. Anna had been a tad luckier than her mother though, she had found a man to love, marry and have a child with. But luck can only run so far. She was taken by a particularly grueling form of cancer at forty-seven. Ol' Jim hadn't really known his father. The man died from a massive heart attack when he was three. So, after his mother died, for a spell it was just Ol' Jim and his Nana. The woman who had given him talent and the courage to use it.

When Martha Baine died, she left her house and all of her belongings to Ol' Jim to do with as he pleased. The house sat idle and gathering dust for years and years, he was unable to bring himself to sell it or go through its inner workings. He had loved his Nana very much and just the thought of stepping into the house's eternal emptiness was too much for him to handle. In those years of loneliness was when Ol' Jim had written *Underneath the Night*—to embrace and prolong her memory.

Years passed, a couple of decades maybe, the house sat still and untouched. Ol' Jim already had a place to live and didn't desperately need the money that selling it would bring him. He liked the idea of it being there, mysterious and dark, something for people to wonder about and the kids to make up ghost stories. But, a little over four months before that night Ol' Jim sang his song at The Warhorse, he had gotten a feverish bout of nostalgia in the middle of the night and just had to go back to that old house.

The house had the look of complete abandonment and smelled as if it were rotting from the inside. All manner of critters had made the house home and hadn't done well at picking up after themselves. Dust seemed to hang in every inch of the air and cobwebs covered every wall. Armed with gloves, a bandana over his mouth, trash bags and several types of chemical based cleaners, Ol' Jim set to work. On the fifth day into cleaning, he sat against a wall and looked around. The house had been restored to a portion of its former glory. He thought he could feel some of the love returning and hear music coming from the rooms.

After going into town for a quick breakfast, he returned and began going through dressers and closets with a renewed sense of determination. By that afternoon he had found photos, cards, jewelry and other keepsakes that had been thought lost forever. Ol' Jim smiled as he traced over photographs of his Nana, mother and uncle. They rarely smiled but always seemed to be happy when near each other.

There was one small bedside dresser left to investigate. It was in a back room, hidden away in a dusty corner away from the windows, as if being protected from the light. He went through it and it was mostly just what he had expected— small knickknacks and trivial items that had really only been important to his grandmother. But then, in the back of a drawer wrapped in cloth, Ol' Jim took out a small book. When he removed the cloth, he discovered it was something like a small journal, bound in aged brown leather with only "WORDS" written on the cover in dark black ink.

Ol' Jim sat back on the floor with child-like curiosity and opened the journal. To his surprise, every page contained a poem or two penned in his Nana's handwriting. He smiled and hugged the book close to his chest, embracing this new remembrance. He leafed through the pages, scanning the words on them quickly until he came across a poem that stopped everything. It was untitled and every word was written in a fast cursive, as if the she had been in a deathly hurry to get this particular poem down on paper . The words came off the page and invaded his soul, warming his core while simultaneously sending chills down his back. It was the most beautiful thing Ol' Jim had ever read.

That same day, after packing up the items he wanted to keep with him and leaving the house behind, Ol' Jim really needed a drink and headed to a dive bar called Sammy's. Beer in hand, he read and reread the poems in the journal. And every time he came across that one poem, he went over it slowly, trying to scrutinize every word and syllable; trying to understand its essence. The third time through the journal, he had several beers in his blood and began reading the poems out loud to himself.

"Keep it down over there," a cantankerous old man sitting at the table directly across from Ol' Jim yelled in his direction. *"Can't a man drink in some goddamn peace and quiet around here?"*

"Sorry," Ol' Jim muttered and drained the beer bottle in front of him.

He made his way to that one poem again and, despite the old man's objections, he read the poem aloud but just barely audible, so that he could hear the words come out of his mouth. After finishing the poem, he smiled and was about to order another beer when the old man in front of him grabbed his chest and gasped for air. Ol' Jim watched as his eyes rolled straight back into his head so all that was visible were orbs of pure white and then the old man fell onto the floor stone dead.

Ol' Jim didn't think much of the incident, other than how swiftly it had happened, until others around him started dropping dead whenever he would go out: young people, healthy people. It took awhile for Jim to realize that this happened whenever he would mumble that poem to himself but when he did the revelation shook him like an earthquake. *'There was no way I caused this,'* he thought to himself, *'there's just no way in hell.'*

Shut up in his apartment for days, Ol' Jim went over every time someone had died while in close proximity to him in the past several weeks. And every time, every goddamn time, it happened just after he had said the poem to himself. He knew that the only thing to do now was to test this, he had to know if this was really what had happened or if it had all been unfortunate timing.

Ol' Jim went out in search of the dirty bum that hung around town. "The Preacher" everyone called the man because he was always quoting the Bible to himself or to anyone that would listen for two seconds. He found the preacher in the alley beside the All Night Diner, rooting through their dumpster for food. The preacher heard Ol' Jim approaching and abruptly ended his search and turned to face him. His eyes shone a deep blue through the dark dirt on his face and the hair that covered them.

"And Cain talked with his brother Abel; and it came to pass, that when they were in the field, Cain rose up against Abel his brother, and slew him," the preacher said unflinching.

Ol' Jim, surprised by the man's words, backed up several steps. However, understanding that he must find out about the power of the poem's words, he said them aloud to the preacher. When he was done, he stood in the alley in silence, waiting. Seconds passed and then suddenly the preacher dropped to his knees, clenched his chest through his disgusting clothes and then fell over onto the pavement. Ol' Jim watched this and then dropped to his own knees, tears in his eyes. He thought about the power that he now possessed and knew what he had to do.

•

Another round of uninhibited applause bounced off the walls as Ol' Jim finished playing. He smiled as hands clapped together in rigorous unison and then grabbed the microphone as the crowd quieted down.

"Thank you, thank you very much. You're too kind." He straightened up on the stool and held Ruby close. "Right now, I'm gonna play something for you that's brand new. Nobody's ever heard it before." A few whistles and cheers sprung up into the air. "It's called *Goodbye.*" Another short round of cheers went out and Ol' Jim started tapping his foot on the floor. A few seconds later he began playing low dark notes in rapid succession; the anticipation was killing him.

There comes a time when we know
We know it's too late to cry
Shout up to god
He ain't listenin' no more

21

Just wantin' to know why
Why we never got to say goodbye
So goodbye, goodbye
So goodbye, goodbye

Ol' Jim sat beside his Nana's bed with Ruby on his lap. He finished playing 'I'll Never Get Out of This World Alive,' his Nana's favorite Hank Williams song and sat there in the silence, looking at her withered body and watching her labored breathing. She turned her head and slowly brought her hand up and urged him to come closer with her pointer finger. Ol' Jim lay Ruby aside and came close to her, so close he could smell death coming off of her.

"Make them remember you," she whispered into his ear and drew away.

He sat stunned and still, watched as she closed her eyes while taking her last breath. After it was over, Ol' Jim sat for awhile before calling the undertaker to come and retrieve the body, wondering what he was going to do without her.

Playing hard and fast through the bridge, Ol' Jim knew that the chorus was coming and was so excited that he was having trouble making his fingers do what he wanted them to. It had taken him awhile to find the music to go perfectly with the words but it had finally come to him in a dream. And then the time was upon him. Ol' Jim opened his mouth and sang the words that he had read over and over again. He listened to them coming out of him, coming from his soul, and he wanted to cry.

When the words were done he kept playing as he scanned the room, watching as the audience—one after the other—grabbed at their chests and fell to the floor. Ol' Jim watched as people who he considered friends, and others he knew, fell to the floor and he imagined watching their souls leave their bodies. He felt a twinge of sadness and regret for them but this passed quickly; it was the price of greatness. The sacrifice for immortality. They were all going to be remembered forever now, just like him.

Ol' Jim slowly put Ruby on the floor and tip-toed over to the phone behind the bar. He had to step over Donny to reach it. After dialing the number, he listened with impatience as the sound of ringing filled his ears, his hands were shaking he was so excited. A woman picked up on the other end.

"Yes, 9-1-1?" He said, unable to mask the glee in his voice. "You need to get over to The Warhorse, immediately." And he hung up the phone.

Walking again past the gauntlet of bodies, Ol' Jim sat back down on the stool and picked Ruby back up. He strummed a few chords and laughed aloud to himself. It was his time now, they would all remember him. Everyone would want to know the secret in his music. He was finally going to be a big time player.

SNOW ON THE MOUNTAIN

It was Blake's snoring that woke Julianne from a pleasant slumber, but it was the cold creeping in from outside that kept her awake. The wind bit fiercely at Julianne through the tent walls, her sleeping bag, and her thermal underwear. Chills went through her body as the shakes prevented her from gaining enough calm to fall back asleep.

Light breaks through the tent, but just barely enough for Julianne to see shadows. Out of the sleeping bag, she crawled to the tent's entrance and unzipped the flap. The coldness she was feeling is now immediate and brutal. Looking around, all Julianne could see was white, everywhere. She smiled and zipped the flap back up quickly.

"Blake," she whispered beside her boyfriend's ear, "get up."

He twitched briefly in his sleeping bag, but continued to snore. Julianne nudged herself close while shaking him slightly.

"Blake," she repeated, a little louder than before.

This time he took in a guttural breath and rolled over. His eyelids let out a furry of blinks as he adjusted them to see her.

"Go back to sleep, Jules," he muttered and plopped his arm across her.

"It's snowing," she said quietly with Blake facing her.

Blake opened his eyes slowly and rubbed them with his free hand, while the hand that was across Julianne's body was cupping her ass. He looked towards the front tent flap as if he would be able to see through its lining.

"What time is it?"

Julianne looked at her watch. "A little after seven."

"Fuck," he said and threw his face back into his pillow, "it's too early."

"Come on, baby, you gotta see," she couldn't hide her excitement, "It's magical."

She kept nudging him until he finally sat up and rubbed his face with his hands, the sign that he was waking up. Reaching beside the sleeping bag, he picked up his glasses and set them haphazardly on his nose; she always thought he looked better with them on. Julianne drew close and kissed him gently on the cheek. Blake smiled as he fumbled out of his sleeping bag.

"Oh, wow," he said quietly after unzipping the tent flap. "That's beautiful."

Julianne joined him and stared as the flakes fell, heavy and round, covering almost everything in sight. They had chosen this spot to camp because it rested under a canopy of large oak trees. So they were protected from the unrelenting downpour. But past the last oak going back down the mountain, nothing could be seen.

"Hey, Mike!" Blake called out unexpectedly. "Y'all awake?"

Mike and Rose's tent was set up several yards down from Julianne and Blake's. Both parties had considered the distance due to carnal pleasures that would undoubtedly take place during the night, neither couple wanting to hear the other.

Julianne watched as the flap of the other tent was slowly unzipped and Mike popped his head out, his shaggy blonde hair ruffled and matted to his face, his eyes wide in surprise.

"Holy shit," he said loud enough to cover the distance. "Rose, get out here."

Within a few seconds Rose appeared, her long black, curly hair tied tight behind her head.

"Oh, my god," she said, scanning over the scene.

"This is something, isn't it?" Julianne called down.

"It's amazing," Rose answered and held her hand out to catch the falling flakes.

Within twenty minutes all four were out of their tents and properly dressed for the bitter cold, under the awning which they had erected over a picnic table and fire pit that was beside Julianne and Blake's tent. Blake tended sausages on a screen over the fire while everyone else sipped hot chocolate and awed at the snow and how much it covered since the previous night.

"Where do you think everybody else is?" Mike asked after taking a big gulp from his cup.

"They probably got scared by the snow and high-tailed it outta here." Blake answered and then snickered.

The two couples had hiked up the mountain a bit further than other campers because Blake knew of this spot under the trees, but there was an actual campground at the foot and they had met a few other campers on their way up. The two previous days the air had been filled with the sounds of yelling, laughter and children playing. But now, all was still. Silence came down with the snow.

"Do you think we should leave, too?" Rose asked. Julianne could hear traces of fear in her voice.

"We're fine, don't worry about it," Blake said as he pulled the sausages off of the screen. "The snow will break sometime today and then tomorrow we'll hike back down to the truck, as planned." He smiled his trusting smile at everyone and served breakfast.

The day was spent eating, drinking, laughing and playing card games. Julianne all the while watched the snow pour down, her child-like sense of awe waning as the hours passed with no sign of the storm breaking.

"What are we gonna do?" She asked Blake in the privacy of their tent as dusk gave way to darkness.

"Relax, hang out. We got enough food to last a couple more days." Blake leaned close and kissed her gently. "It can't snow forever."

Julianne looked toward the closed tent flap as Blake opened another beer. She could still hear the gentle sound of the flakes falling on top of one another.

The night was filled with little sleep and nothingness where dreams should have been. Julianne woke before the sun and felt the coldness biting at her once again. Rolled up tight in her sleeping bag, she lay listening to Blake's snoring and waited patiently for the first morning rays to break through the tent.

"Blake," she whispered beside her boyfriend's ear, "get up."

Julianne nudged him several times but he would not be stirred. Weary and tired from the restless night, she crawled to the tent flap and unzipped it.

"Ah," Julianne gasped almost inaudibly as the morning air wrapped around her and she looked over the vast whiteness that had taken over almost everything in sight.

"Blake, get up." This time she used more volume and authority.

Blake rolled over to face her and blinked rapidly. "What is it?"

"I can't see anything." Even she could hear the panic in her voice.

He sat up and rubbed his face in his hands. "What are you talking about, babe?"

27

"There's nothing out there."

Blake's gaze hardened as if he didn't know what to make of the statement. He put on his glasses, untangled himself from the sleeping bag and crawled to join Julianne. Together, they peered out into the snow. The flakes were still falling with no end in sight and, sure enough, nothing could be seen outside a foot from the tent, only white. Not even the trees were protecting them now.

"Mike!" Blake called out after a few seconds.

"Rose!" Julianne followed suit.

They waited, hearing nothing but the silence echoing back at them.

"Rose!" Julianne bellowed again.

"I'm going out there," Blake said and grabbed his pants and jacket.

"What do you mean? You can't go out there."

"What are you talking about? Of course I can." Blake pulled up his pants and went about putting on his boots.

"No, Blake," Julianne grabbed his arm, "you can't."

"Jules, what's wrong with you? What if they need help?" He finished with his boots and threw his jacket around his arms.

"They're not out there!"

Blake turned to face her, bending down on his knees so they were at the same level. "I have to go see if they need help," he said with a strange calm.

"I'm telling you, they're not there." Julianne said quietly and let out a sob.

"Of course they're there!"

"Just look! They're gone!" She was yelling but didn't care. "Everything's gone!" The tears came then with reckless abandon.

Blake took her in his arms and Julianne let herself fall into them, weeping into his shoulder. They stayed this way for a minute before he pulled himself away while still holding onto her arms.

"It's ten feet away," he said, wiping the hair away from her eyes. "I'll be back in a flash."

Julianne clutched him and pulled him into another embrace. "Please," she whispered beside his ear, "don't go." She was unable to stop herself from trembling.

Blake pulled himself away once more, smiled and then kissed her gently. "Everything's going to be ok." He zipped up his coat and stepped out into the snow.

Julianne watched the back of his jacket disappear into the white, knowing that would be the last time she would see him. A few minutes went by, an hour, two hours; time seemed not to matter after that.

"Blake!" She yelled out into the distance, knowing she would get no answer but needing to try anyway.

She screamed until her voice cracked and throat ached. The snow continued to fall and Julianne sat wrapped in her sleeping bag staring as it inched closer and closer to her. All that was left now was the sound of her crying reverberating off of the tent walls.

HORSEMEN

"Tell me about the fire."

The therapist says this with a blank expression, clearly practiced at being non-judgmental to any answer that is given. Or at least showing any on her face.

Sean McClarity stares at her from a large, stereotypical, black leather sofa ten paces from her matching arm chair. He remembers setting foot for the first time in the office two weeks ago and being amused by her lack of creativity.

"The fire, Sean?"

Her frown lines show through an otherwise smooth face, darkened by the sun and wrinkled by time. Looking into her dimming blue eyes, the heat is coming back to Sean's face. He can feel his lungs being polluted once again with black, putrid smoke, not letting him breathe.

"I don't remember much."

On his knees, on his front lawn, Sean could smell the burning—the burning of wood, of fabric, of grass and of flesh. As he watched his house and everything he owned being consumed by a force he couldn't compete with, Sean thought that he should be crying. He should be angry. He should be going to the ambulance that's parked in the middle of the street with its sirens blazing. But all he could do was slump on his knees, in his yard, and stare through the orange and red hue of the flames that were destroying his world, to the painting that hung on his kitchen wall.

Sean imagined the canvas bubbling up and the paint running, dripping down onto the burning hardwood. And then the flames were upon it, singeing its design and crumbling its essence. This was the end, Sean knew, and there was nothing that he could do about it.

Φ

Two days after the fire Sean was sleeping in his old room at his mother's house and dreaming of a lake made of glass. Stepping onto it, Sean could see his reflection but the face wasn't his. Smiling back at Sean was a grin made up of pointed teeth that went sideways up his right cheek. The stranger's eyes were completely white, reminding Sean of death. The stranger nodded forward toward the center of the lake and when Sean looked up the glass was cracking, dissolving into a jagged circle with black fire rising up from the opening. A ringing ruptured the air around Sean and the ground began to shake. After a few seconds the ringing stopped and Sean began walking towards the opening and the flames. The ringing thundered again and, this time, Sean fell to his knees. He watched the glass began to splinter around him and felt the immense fear that he would soon be swallowed by it.

Sean was awakened by the third ring of the telephone. Lying on top of the covers of his perfectly made bed, Sean felt two things immediately: The throbbing in his temples and the stinging sensation of the burns on his hands and forearms. Bringing himself up to a sitting position on the bed—with some degree of difficulty, due to the fact that he couldn't put any pressure on his arms—Sean looked at his bandages. They looked wet and were stuck to his skin because of the grease from the ointment and the oozing from his wounds. It had been a few hours since his wounds had been cleaned. Soon his mother would have to help him wash his arms and hands, scrubbing them to keep them clear of infection (which to Sean feels a bit like being burned all over again) and re-bandage them. *Second degree burns, what luck,* thought Sean.

There was a light knock at the door which was soon followed by his mother opening the door slightly and sticking her head through the opening.

"Sean?" She said in almost a whisper.

"Yea, Mom." The light from the hallway seemed blinding to Sean even though it was a dim bulb. The throbbing in his head continued and a bit of nausea arose in his stomach.

"There's someone on the phone for you."

"Okay."

Sean extended his hand and his mother eased the door open a bit more and walked through it, coming only close enough so the cordless phone could reach to Sean's hand and retreating after he had taken it.

"Mom, could you find my pain meds for me?"

"Sure." She replied in a polite manner that seemed to Sean more suitable for house guests than injured sons.

"Hello?" Sean said into the phone after a few seconds of fidgeting with it, trying to get a good grip without hurting his hands.

"Hello, Sean." The voice glided through the receiver and the surprise caught the nausea in Sean's stomach and brought it up to his throat, almost expelling it all over his sheets.

"Hello, Cara." Sean managed to whisper, thinking he was talking to a ghost. In that second he imagined the apparition on the other side of the phone hovering in some parallel universe. The ability to time travel through a phone.

"Well," she gave a slight giggle, "I didn't think you'd remember."

Sean's mouth was dry and his attempts to bring saliva to lips were in vain. His throat felt scratchy and speaking was difficult.

"I didn't think I could forget."

"Did you try?" Her voice lost the girlish tone it had a second ago and adopted a more serious one.

"Apparently not hard enough."

The silence that followed was worse than Sean's headache. *What the fuck do you want?* is all that Sean wanted to say—to yell—at her but, even after all this time, he still couldn't find the anger.

"Are you okay? I heard about the fire."

"I'm alive." He said with a distant tone. *That's right, Sean, play it cool.*

"But are you *okay*?"

Sean was unable to make sense of the concern in her voice. After a woman chases you around an apartment with a butcher's knife, stabbing wildly through the air, you figure she's lost all concern for your well being. Admittedly, though, the incident had been Sean's fault.

"Second degree burns on my hands and arms. But other than that I'm fine."

"That's good to hear." Her sincerity was severely throwing him off and Sean was fighting to keep from losing his composure when she spoke.

"How did you get my Mother's number," he managed to say after a long pause. "It's not listed."

"I remembered it from that month you stayed with her when you were looking for a place to live."

Sean could almost see her lips curling in a satisfied smile from displaying her prowess. That had been over three years ago and she still remembered the number; even though he didn't want to be, Sean was impressed.

"I…" Cara began but there was a pause and Sean decided to beat her to the punch.

"I don't have it."

"Oh." Her tone made it sound like she wanted to hear more but another pause followed.

"It was in the house." Sean waited expectantly for her reply.

"Is that why you got burned?" It was not what Sean was expecting and again he could hear concern.

"Yes."

"Oh," she said with what sounded like a hint of sadness. "I'm sorry you got hurt trying to save…which one did you have again?"

Sean took a deep breath. "The Four Who Ride," he said as calmly as possible.

"Oh, yes, you did always like that one." Cara's voice shifted to a lighter tone. Sean kept imagining her small, curled smile.

"You used to love it." His tone was cold and biting.

"I use to love a lot of things." Another shift, hers bit harder.

There was almost half a minute of silence with neither wanting to break the barrier, neither wanting to reproach the frost.

"Well, like I said, it's gone now so nothing's keeping you here."

There was another slight pause. "I'm not going anywhere, Sean."

"Why not?" Sean blurted out the question with surprise before he had a chance to think.

"Because I don't want to kill myself anymore."

Sean let his mouth hang open with her revelation but was unable to find the words, unable to think.

Cara broke the silence: "You held on to that painting for so long…things have changed." More silence. This is nothing like what Sean had imagined. "I'm happy now." Her voice sounded so lively and full of hope; Sean felt nausea pains rising in his stomach and really wished his mom would hurry back with his pills. "How about we get together," she continued, "for dinner or something." Another pause. "When you're feeling better."

"Sure," Sean said through bile and acid that were burning his throat. "When I'm feeling better."

"Good," Sean could still imagine her smile. "Good-bye, Sean."

"Good-bye, Cara."

The phone went dead on the other end and Sean sat there listening to it, trying to go over what just happened in his mind but then remembered his headache. Finally, Sean hung up the phone, collapsed onto his back and closed his eyes.

Φ

The therapist scribbles something onto her pad and resumes her stare at Sean. Sitting leg over leg, Sean thinks she resembles a tiger getting ready to pounce and the sound from the tip of her pointed shoe tapping against the leg of her chair is deafening in the silence.

"So, how long were you with this girl?"

"Uh…about a year and a half," Sean says, happy to have the silence broken.

"And you've been apart for how long now?"

"A little over two years."

The therapist looks up from her pad and seems to examine Sean thoroughly with her eyes. *What the fuck is she looking for?* Sean asks himself. He has never been a fan of being scrutinized, therapy wasn't his idea.

"How would you describe that relationship?"

"Uh..." Sean racks his brain to find the right word, "tumultuous." *There it is.*

"Well, that's quite an adverb," she scribbles some more. "So, why were you together for so long?

Well, that's quite the question Sean thinks and wishes he could come up with an answer, a real answer besides the one he was going to give. "I thought I was in love with her."

"And you don't think that now?"

"It's hard to say."

There is more scribbling. The sound of pen on paper is beginning to hurt Sean's eardrums.

"Do you think she's part of the reason that you didn't finish school?"

Sean takes in a deep breath and lets it out slowly. "Possibly."

No scribbles this time, the therapist simply takes off her glasses and cleans them on a cloth from her pocket. Sean wonders if this has some hidden meaning in it. "Well, then, let's start at the beginning, shall we? How did you two meet?"

Sean remembers the cold and how his hair stuck to his face. He remembers the bleak turning into the intolerable, and then a mesmerizing shade of green that he had never seen before.

Φ

Shuffling his feet with rain blinding his every step, Sean had no idea where he was going on campus, just that he was going. He felt every drop of rain that drenched his body and each one weighed him down that much more. One foot after the other, rain drop after rain drop, Sean was moving ever closer to oblivion.

And then, without warning, the rain ceased bombarding Sean from above. He continued shuffling his feet but looked up and could see the rain still drowning the Earth in front of him and could hear splashing sounds against the umbrella which now covered his head. Sean felt her before she spoke.

"Thought you could use some shelter." Sean didn't know the voice but it sounded as if it could make time stop, if it wanted to.

Sean came to halt and turned to see her face: She had long auburn hair tied back in a pony tail and fiercely green eyes which contrasted to the point of perfection with her smooth, pale skin. She must have noticed the look on Sean's cold, soaked face because her eyes saddened and seemed to dim. Sean never wanted to make them look that way again.

"What's wrong?" She asked with more concern than Sean knew someone could have for a complete stranger.

Sean let out an exhausted breath and suddenly couldn't tell if his face was just wet or if he had been crying. "My..." Sean began but didn't know if he wanted to continue. He didn't know this girl, this beautiful girl, and definitely didn't think that she could help. But, looking into her eyes, watching them overflow with worry for him, Sean suddenly wanted to tell her everything—tell her everything without even knowing her name. "My dad just died."

The beautiful girls' eyes widened and her lips parted slightly as if she had something to say but she didn't speak. There wasn't anything to say, really. With her free hand she grabbed Sean's shoulder, pulled him close and wrapped her arm tightly around his neck. Sean put his arms around her and felt her warmth in the freezing rain. In her embrace, nuzzled close to her, Sean felt safe.

After a minute she withdrew but kept her free hand on Sean's shoulder; he wanted it to stay there forever. "I'm Cara," she said with tears in her eyes.

"I'm Sean."

"Well, Sean, now that we've met I would feel horrible if you caught pneumonia," she said with a sad little smile. "Come on, let's get you inside and dry."

Φ

"And that was it," Sean says in a very matter-of-fact way, like he's reading it from a book.

"So, she helped you get through your father's death?" The therapist asks with seemingly very little interest as she scribbles.

"Yes," Sean barely gets the answer out. As much as he doesn't want to admit it, if it hadn't of been for me her he never would've made it.

"Were you close with your father, Sean?"

"Close enough, I guess," Sean thinks back as he talks. "I was closer with my mother but we had our bonds, mostly over sports but it seemed to be enough."

"How did your mother take his passing?"

"They had been divorced for a few years when it happened but it hit her pretty hard," Sean can't hide the frown that covers his face. "She hit the bottle for awhile. She's way better now but still drinks more than she wants to admit."

"You're living with her now, aren't you?"

"Just until I'm back on my feet."

"And how's that going?"

"It's difficult," Sean says after a pause. The next few moments are silent except for when the pen is on the paper. *That damn pen, criticizing my every word* Sean thinks to himself. His arms itch but he can't scratch them.

"So, what happened with you and Cara after that night?"

38

"We went for coffee." She stops scribbling and Sean smiles—he's know what she's asking and he knows that he's being difficult but it amuses him. "We barely left each other's side after that," he continues, "for a year we were inseparable."

More scribbling. "Why did that change?"

Sean sighs, preferring not to think about it. *It will help you to talk about it* everyone keeps saying to him. *It fucking better* Sean thinks. "I guess the trouble started when she graduated. I had partied and slept enough to be a year off track but she was finishing on time—with her bachelors of fine arts degree, in painting. She did just about everything: Painting, drawing, sculpting and even a little welding. She had planned to move back home with her family after she was done but we really didn't want to do the long distance thing." Sean stops to gather his thoughts.

"Go on."

Sean let's out another long sigh. "We found this place together and everything was good for a little while. I was still doing my school thing and she had really dived into her paintings—sometimes working for a couple of days straight. I think that's where the stress started. She was trying to get enough of what she considered "great work" so that she could try and get into a gallery to get her name out there."

"Stress can do quite a number on relationships."

Sean laughs, "Yea, tell me about it." *That's some fucking insight you got there, lady.* "We stopped having fun and talking to each other. We became just people who lived together instead of people who were in love."

"Is that when you decided to break it off?"

"No, that was, uh…" Sean chuckles to himself. "No, that was a few months later. She finally got to a point where she felt like she could start showing her work and things got better:

We spent time together, laughed, shared our lives and were basically a couple again. Almost like nothing had ever been wrong."

"What happened to change that?"

The therapist has stopped writing things down and Sean really feels like she is listening now. Taking a deep breath, Sean shivers slightly before continuing, "The rejection letters started coming. One after the other, every place that she had submitted her paintings to. It was like an avalanche of bad news that never stopped."

"Was she not a good artist?"

Sean turns his head to stare the therapist in her eyes, feeling almost as if she had insulted him in some fashion. "She was fantastic. The ways she used colors and shading and shapes… it was the best art I have ever seen."

"Are you sure you weren't just biased because of how you felt about her?"

It is a stinging question and Sean retreats a bit, slumping against the back of the couch. "I don't know," Sean says and turns his head away from her eyes.

"Continue."

Sean doesn't want to talk anymore but he's paying for this session and there's still half an hour left. He was raised not to waste money. "Living with her was like being in a war zone: Everything I said and everything I did was like stepping on a landmine or getting shot in the ass. Finally, after three months of rejection letters, she decided that she was done."

"With painting?"

Sean takes another breath and exhales slowly. "With living." He turns back to face the therapist. She's tilted her head slightly and there is a questioning look on her face. "She said that she had put her entire essence and being into those paintings," Sean continues, "they were her soul. And if no one could see and understand that, than neither they nor she needed to exist."

"Well, that's quite a statement."

Sean chuckles quietly to himself. "Yes, it is."

"What did you do?"

"I told her that I loved her paintings, as much as I loved her. That all of her friends loved her and her paintings and that we all understood what they meant to her. But she didn't care. She was too blinded by rage and sadness to hear anything." Sean takes a breath and starts to fight against tears that he can feel forming. "In the end, she said that my love was meaningless. She said the only love she had ever felt for me had come from pity, because of the night we met, and it was time for me to deal with that and move on because she wasn't gonna be around anymore." Sean loses his struggle and tears start to come. He blinks wildly to keep them from getting into his eyes and finally uses the back of his hand to wipe them away completely.

"What did you do?"

"Oh, I completely lost it," Sean says and sniffs, "we had a huge yelling match for about three hours until she finally just stormed out."

"Was that the last time you saw her?"

"No, the next night was."

"What happened then?"

"She chased me around with a butcher knife."

"Well," the therapist says with surprise in her voice, "that certainly sounds dramatic."

Sean laughs so hard that he begins to cough. "Yea," he says after he composes himself.

"Why did she do that?"

"Because I stole one of her paintings," Sean says in a low voice. "She had left behind the keys to her storage unit where her paintings were so I went in the middle of the night and stole one."

The therapist has another puzzled look on her face. "Why would you steal one of her paintings?"

"Because she said that, before she killed herself, she had to get rid of her paintings," Sean says, not looking into the therapist's eyes. "That every last, little piece of her soul had to be destroyed before she could be at peace."

Φ

Sean noticed that the door to the apartment was slightly open and instantly knew that Cara was in there. Pushing the door open easily with his fingertips, Sean stuck his head in and looked around the living room: The couch and loveseat were empty, the papasan in the corner—nothing. Sean slid into the room and closed the door, barely making a sound. He knew she was there somewhere.

Moving slowly and on his toes, Sean started to walk toward the hallway that led to the kitchen and then to the bedroom, but then stopped. On the table sitting against the half wall that separated the living room and the kitchen—the table where he and Cara shared countless meals together—there was a painting. Sean silently slinked over to the table to get a better look. The painting depicted the figure of a person, bundled in winter clothes, standing on a lake against the backdrop of a dreary grey sky. In the middle of the lake, in front of the person, there was a hole with ice going up around it that looked like shards of glass. And rising from the hole were black shapes, not puffy and dull like smoke but sharp and fierce, like fire.

Sean stared at the painting for what seemed like an eternity—Cara had named it "Treading Thin Fire"—when he heard the sudden sound of a drawer closing. Looking up from the painting, Sean saw Cara stand up in the kitchen from behind the half wall, holding a particularly large butcher's knife.

"You thieving, motherfucking, piece of shit," Cara exclaimed as their eyes locked on one another. "What did you do with it?"

Staring into the eyes of madness, "Hey," is all that Sean could think to say.

"Where is it?" Fury lit up her eyes.

"Where is what?"

"Don't play dumb, Sean, where is my painting? You stole it from my storage unit."

Sean just stared at the knife in her hand, raised up so he could see her face reflected in its blade; he wasn't sure which version of her looked angrier. "It's safe."

"Safe?!"

Cara stomped through the kitchen and into the living room. Sean moved back to put at least the coffee table between them while Cara stood beside the table with the painting. "You know that it has to go."

"I won't let you do it."

"Won't let me?" The fury seemed to grow. "It belongs to me—I created it and now I'm going to destroy it."

"I'm not giving it back."

"I'll find it."

"Doubtful," Sean said with wavering assurance as Cara raised the knife in the air.

"Well, then," she said as she pointed the knife at Sean.

And then, without warning, Cara moved quickly over to the table and brought the knife down with more force than

Sean knew she had into the middle of the painting. She dragged the knife up and then down and then, bringing the knife back out, she slashed it across the middle making the cuts resemble a cross. Sean watched as Cara brought a small container out of her jeans pocket. When she started squirting its contents onto what was left of the painting, Sean realized it was lighter fluid.

"Cara, no."

She raised the knife and pointed at him again as he stepped closer. Then she pulled a book of matches from the same pocket, lit one and dropped it onto the painting. Flames rose immediately from the table, creating an eerie shadow that seemed to dance wickedly on the walls. Sean thought of the person in the painting and thought that he smelled flesh burning and then realized it was all in his mind.

"You see," Cara said as Sean watched the fire consume the canvas, "there's only one left, now. The sooner you give it to me, the sooner I'm out of your life."

Sean lifted his head to look at her face: It was cold and expressionless. A far cry from the face that he had fell in love with. "No."

Cara's right eye twitched and her mouth moved into what Sean could only perceive as a half snarl and before he knew what was happening she was moving towards him. Walking across the coffee table, she lunged at him with the knife extended. Suddenly aware of the situation, Sean quickly moved out of the way as Cara went past him and fell to the floor. Getting back to her feet, she turned around and swung the knife in Sean's direction. Again he moved and the blade plunged into one of the couch cushions. Sean took a few backward steps toward the kitchen as Cara withdrew the blade and followed him.

"Cara..." he said as she inched closer towards him, watching the knife as she walked.

Cara advanced at Sean and again swung the knife through the air. This time Sean took a side step and, when she was off balance, pushed her into the wall. She hit with a thud and a groan as Sean raced by her and into the kitchen, quickly jerked open the cabinet doors below the sink and retrieved the fire extinguisher. As Cara entered the kitchen Sean stood up and aimed the nozzle of the extinguisher at her.

"Really, Sean?" She said with a smile on her face.

"Cara, this is crazy," Sean pleaded with her.

Before she could take another step toward him the smoke alarm began to blare its warning in a deafening manner. Sean sighed. The superintendent would be alerted and come check to see what was happening. Cara looked around, then back at Sean and began to back away slowly.

"This isn't finished," she said as she kept moving toward the door.

"Yes, it is," Sean said from behind the half wall of the kitchen.

Cara blinked and then a strange, small smile crept across her face. "I'll see you in hell," she said, dropped the knife, turn and ran out the door.

Sean took a deep breath to calm himself. Then, feeling the heat and remembering the fire, he aimed the nozzle at the burning table and unloaded the contents of the extinguisher.

Φ

"So, you didn't see her again after that?" The therapist asks in a slightly less monotone voice than she had been using.

"No," Sean says then takes a breath. "Not until after the fire at my house."

"And how did that go?"

"Oh, it was fine." Sean drops his head, closes his eyes and rubs his temples. He can feel the beginning of a headache.

"She was no longer concerned with the painting that you stole?"

"Nope," Sean says without looking up.

"Did she say why?"

Sean lets out a long sigh. "She said that she had met someone who helped her discover who she needed to be and paint what she needed to paint. Apparently, her paintings are doing quite well now."

There is a momentary pause from the therapist. "And how did that make you feel?"

Sean looks up at the question and into her eyes. "I didn't feel anything."

She tilts her head down to her notepad and does some more scribbling. "Will you describe the painting that you took from her for me?" She asks after she finishes.

Sean closes his eyes again and sits back against the couch. "It was dark," he begins, picturing it in his head, "like just before nightfall on a dreary day—that sort of perfect blend between black and grey. Then from the middle, you see four horses, just outlines really, and yet so detailed. It's just their fronts, like they're going to jump right out at you. Their faces and necks look like regular horses but the sternums and front legs are completely skeletal." Sean stops to catch his breath.

"Go on," the therapist urges.

"On each horse is a figure, barely even an outline, and they appear to only be wearing black robes but, under the black hoods, there are no faces. There is just darkness, except small, dark red orbs that are evil and seem to pierce the soul." Sean takes another breath. "And under their hoofs they were kicking up a large cloud of grey dust that flows and disappears into the darkness behind them. She called it 'The Four Who Ride.'"

Sean stops and wipes away a tear that had crawled out from behind his closed eye lid and then opened his eyes again.

"Did you have some sort of emotional connection to that painting before this all happened?"

"No, I had just always liked to look at it. But afterwards, I guess...I guess I could understand its dread, the impending doom that came with it." Sean laughs and wipes away another tear. "My own personal apocalypse."

"Now, Sean, I know you're hesitant to talk about it but I want you to tell me about the fire," the therapist begins in a coaxing tone, "if you can."

Sean ruffles his already messed up hair with his hands and takes a deep breath. *This has been the longest fucking hour of my life* he thinks and then sighs.

"You don't have to, but I think it would help."

Sean looks over to her into the blue of her eyes and they seem to be gentler now, more caring. *Weird*, Sean thinks. "My mother had come over to cook me dinner, we had been doing this for a few months—she would come over and we would have 'family time,'" Sean used air quotes because they barely spoke when his mother came over and never about anything important. "Anyway, she put a ham in the oven and we were watching TV, waiting for it to cook. And by watching TV I mean I was spacing out and she was guzzling her whiskey and coke which she thought I didn't know had whiskey in it."

"Why do you think she's hiding her drinking from you?"

"She's not hiding the drinking, what she's trying to hide is how much."

"I see," was all that she said.

Sean waits to see if she is going to say anything else before he continues. "Well, apparently my mother had left a kitchen towel over a burner that was still on and it caught fire."

47

"Did the smoke alarm not go off?"

"No," Sean chuckles lightly to himself, "no, the batteries had died a day or two before and I hadn't gotten around to replacing them yet." The therapist gives a slight nod but says nothing. "By the time I smelled the smoke and went into the kitchen," Sean continues, "the stove was already basically engulfed and the fire was moving to the cabinets above the stove where I kept my liquor collection."

"What did you do then?"

"What did I do then? I calmly told mother what was happening and said we should go outside. She didn't believe me when I told her—I could tell she was already almost smashed by the way she looked at me. So, she put down her drink and went to look in the kitchen. When she saw the fire she turned around and ran for the door screaming 'We gotta get the fuck outta here.'" Sean laughs at the memory.

"And you followed her out?"

"Yea, I called 911 when we were out on the lawn watching my house burn."

"And then you remembered the painting was inside?"

"No, actually, it was a few minutes before I thought about it."

"So, when you did, you ran back inside?"

Sean sighed and felt his temples beginning to throb; he lowered his head and rubbed his temples with his fingers, wanting this session to be over.

"Sean?" She asks, clearly wanting him to keep talking.

"I remembered that the painting was still in the house and I started to walk towards it," Sean begins, not lifting his head. "My mother caught up with me and asked what I was doing. When I told her I had to go back in to get the painting she pleaded with me to forget about it, to let it go. I just kept going and she threw her arms around me. I basically dragged her with me until I was in front of the door and then I shrugged her off of me." Sean sighs as he decides what to say. "She went to reach for me again and I threw my hand up. It hit her in the face."

"You struck your mother?"

Sean looks up at the accusation. "I didn't mean to." Sean feels another tear start to form at the corner of his eye. "At least, I don't think I did."

"And how has that affected your relationship with her?"

"She's afraid of me," Sean says and lets the tear roll down his face.

There is silence for a few moments while the therapist writes in her notebook. "Tell me, where was the painting in the house?" She asks when she's done.

"On the kitchen wall, over the table where I eat," Sean lets out a breath. "I liked to look at it in the mornings." The therapist just nods again but says nothing. "When I got in the fire had already swallowed most of the kitchen and was spreading quickly. I saw the flames then, creeping up the wall, threatening to eat the painting. I ran over to it, kicked the crumbling table out of the way and reached for it." Sean stops, recalling the way the fire felt on his arms as he tried to get the painting down.

"But it was too late?"

Sean sniffs and shakes his head several times. "It was too late."

The therapist scribbles some more on her pad and then looks up to the clock on the other side of the office. "Well, we're almost out of time, Sean, but I just wanted to say that was a very brave thing that you did."

Sean looks up slowly at her with bewilderment. "Brave?"

"Yes, brave," she says as she puts the pen and paper down on her desk. "To go into that fire to get her painting, sacrificing yourself to save what you thought was the last piece of her. It's a very brave thing to do for someone you care about." Sean just stares at her as she stares at him, unaware of what to say. "Well," she says and stands from her chair, "That will do it for today."

Sean stands from the couch and walks over to the therapist and shakes her hand. "Wonderful progress," she says and shakes his head thoroughly.

Sean just nods his head and shakes her hand. "I'll see ya next week."

Sean walks out of the door to the building and into the gently breezing autumn air. Once in the parking lot he takes a cigarette from the pack in his pocket and lights it. Inhaling the smoke and nicotine and whatever else is in a cigarette, Sean lets out a little chuckle that is just for him. *Well, she was mostly right* he thinks.

What the therapist couldn't know—what only Sean knew—was the real reason for why he stole the painting. It wasn't out of love, it wasn't to try and save Cara from herself. Sean took the painting so that she couldn't destroy them all, so that her soul would never be at rest. Sean wanted her have the feeling of eternal failure, something she would never be able to be rid of no matter how long she lived. But most of all he wanted her failure to eat away at her soul and he wanted her to go to the grave knowing that he had won—her own personal apocalypse.

"Death is natural and necessary, but not just. It is a random force of nature; survival is equally accidental. Each loss is an occasion to remember that survival is a gift."

~Harriet McBryde Johnson

SURVIVAL RATE

Beep. Cough. Beep. Gag. These are sounds that lives are reduced to. Wearing non-slip hospital booties and opened backed gowns that show your ass while you walk around in a drug induced stupor. Color me embarrassed.

Two days ago, when I regained consciousness, I was drowning in fear. Thrashing against the current in my newly adorned backless gown, a male orderly and a homely nurse were victims of my booties. The attending doctor said that I apologized but God only knows. Morphine laced blood scurrying through my veins I can only imagine the slobbering apologetic grunts and squeals that tumbled forth. Me being naked under my gown and bearing what I perceived as my sorrow. Pathetic.

My attending physician tells me to get exercise by walking up and down the hallway at least once every few hours. So, gathering up my strength and holding tight to my I.V. stand, I hobble around the hospital with people watching me as if I am a wounded, lost puppy. On these trips, I am lulled into an almost catatonic state by the melodies of heart monitors and life support machines. Every moment is a near death experience. But that could be the drugs talking for me as I try to accomplish the task at hand.

Let's go back to why I'm here, that's the story you want: It was night, there were four of us. Headlights are the last thing I remember. Well, that and the smell of gasoline mixed with concrete and urine, but that came after. Maybe the piss was mine, I can't be too sure. Flash forward back to the thrashing. That's my real first memory of after the crash. And a number of orderlies and nurses first impression of me. Well, maybe second. I'm not sure if people really have an opinion of an unconscious, horribly battered seventeen year old boy. If they do, I hope it's "you poor thing." It would certainly make me feel better about the whole kicking thing. Ok, so maybe I wasn't horribly battered. Moderate at best. I just want your sympathy. Color me needy.

Flash forward to me waking up late that first morning when my father accidentally left the newspaper in my room. We had made the front page.

"Drunk Driver Kills Three in Head On Collision." The words said that the drunk driver and I were the only two to survive. He, however, was in intensive care and had yet to wake up. I sat on my bed, staring at the words on the page. Staring through them to their implications. We are entangled together in eternity now. And in a week, after everyone has forgotten about us, we will stay this way forever in the grungy basement of the up-town library. If this is my fifteen minutes I'd like a time machine so I can go back a few hours and drive faster.

There was a sub-article that was attached to mine, one about the importance of wearing a seat-belt. It said that sixty-three percent of people that died in automobile accidents were not wearing their seat-belts. Sixty-three percent. I guess the other thirty-seven percent were just severely unlucky. I wonder what the statistics of my crash would do to that number. There are four people in a car; three are wearing their seat-belts. The car is plowed into on the driver side by a large truck that is going around fifty miles per hour. The three wearing their seat-belts are killed; the driver survives. What kind of fucked up survival rate is that? Color me miraculous.

Josh Boyd. That's his name. It even sounds murderous. He is twenty-four and was reported leaving Smokey's Bar and

Grille at 1:15 in the morning after a heavy drinking session. Friends say Boyd seemed forlorn and distant over a recent break-up and was throwing back whiskey sours like they were fucking lemonade. And my friends wonder—wait, correction, wondered—why I don't drink.

Joyce. Dean. Carl. These are names that should forever be sown into his brain. Theirs are faces that shall forever be etched into mine. The world robbed of Carl the undiscovered prop comedian. Dean the thespian. Joyce the comic book artist. I am the only one that will know of the love shared by Joyce and Dean. Neither of their parents knew they were together. Most of what they experienced—holding hands, joking, laughing, kissing and other things—died in that car. Now it is my job to carry on the remnants. I'd prefer not to be tied down to one career.

Flash forward to the first time I've cried since I was ten. Standing over my mother's freshly dug grave, I can still remember the warmth of the tears on my cheeks fighting against the bitter December chill. What I can't remember is if I was crying more for losing my mother or being left with my father. Oh well, that's another story. The tears I cried now felt vaguely similar—was I crying because my friends died or that I lived? That's the story untold.

When my father came back to the room an hour or two later tears were still tattooed on my cheeks. He asked what was wrong and I swear to fucking Christ I saw actual concern in his eyes. Again, this could be the morphine talking but I hadn't touched the button in a while. No, I believe I saw love inside those green, sullen, alcoholic eyes.

"I gotta tell you, son," he let out an intense old man sigh as he plopped down into the chair beside my bed, "I was really, really scared when I got that call."

His words were slurred. Lunch was what he said he was going to get, I think he found it in liquid form. Maybe it was love in his eyes, maybe it was gin. As long as it kept him quiet I didn't really care which. But still, love would be a nice switch.

"And when they told me that you had been rushed to the hospital," he coughed, swallowed and blinked his eyes three times at me, "I threw my drink down, hopped in the car and sped all the way here." Pause. I think he was looking for appreciation. Color me surprised. "The whole time, I was praying that you would be alright."

"Are you drunk?"

It's all I could muster to ask. I couldn't tell you if I hated him or the alcohol more at the moment. But the way his eyes looked terrified for me; it was so new, and loving, and frightening. I realigned my field of vision with the bed sheets.

"I had a drink or two at lunch," the tremble in his voice reverberated off the walls, "but I'm not drunk."

"Forget about it. I didn't mean anything by it."

My eyes stayed fixated on my feet under the blanket at the end of the bed, my toes sticking out and creating shadows like a perverse mountain range.

Flash forward to the police interview. This was later that same day. The one with the mustache, he was a detective. I could tell by the suit. The other was from vice, I could tell by the uniform and the smell of sweat mixed with desperation. The mustache asked the questions; sweaty and desperate took notes.

"What were you doing out so late?" The mustache twitched.

"I was fucking driving, douche bag. "

I heard the scratching of led on paper. Let the record show that, yes indeed, I called the detective "douche bag."

"Why weren't you wearing your seat-belt?"

"I fucking forgot to put it on."

"There's no need to be defensive." The mustache's tone was hinting at something beyond his statement and I looked over just in time to see the other one cock his eyebrow at me.

"Had you been drinking?" The detective knocked some sort of crumb from his mustache that I had obviously been staring at.

"Honestly, is this how you treat the *victim* of a drunk driver? Should I request that a lawyer be present?"

"There's no need to be defensive," sweaty and desperate echoed the detective in tone and stopped scratching on the paper. "This is all just standard." His left eye drooped downward as I held his powder blue gaze. I had the sudden desire to take that pencil of his and stick into that drooping eye.

"I'm sorry. I'm just a little cranky in the afternoon when I find out from a newspaper that the only people I care about are dead."

My words hang heavy in the air, mingling with the silence it makes the room hot and it's harder to breathe. I want a shower. I hope my father wasn't paying attention to that last bit but I'd rather not look at his face to see.

After the policemen finish with their oh-so-routine questioning, just my father and I are left in the room. Left in the silence. Neither one of us knowing what to say or what to do next. Both of us left with the understanding that what's left might not be enough. I watched him get up and leave without a sound. His shoes didn't even squeak on the floor. I wanted to call out after him. I wanted to ask him to stay, to say *Father, don't leave me.* I didn't want to be alone, that I understood. What I didn't understand, what I couldn't understand, is why I wanted *him* to be in the room with me. My chest began to burn and I knew that it wasn't from the bruising caused by my air bag. Color me heart-broken.

Flash forward to that night while darkness hung in the air like a thick layer of smog and blanketed the entire room with a suffocating sadness. I lie in my bed, attempting to sleep even though I knew the morphine dreams would do nothing to help the situation. I had given up on the lulling insignificance of television programming hours before. When there is nothing else to do it's easy to get lost in the mundane ramblings of thirty-something sitcom stars stuck into carrying on two separate lives. I began to wonder which one seemed more real to them and which one they preferred.

As my breathing began to slow and my eyelids gained weight, the deafening creak of my door opening burst through the black and ruptured the hopes of me ever getting to sleep. I sat up in my bed and stared at the silhouette in the doorway, illuminated slightly by the light in the hallway. I recognized the tall, slim figure with ruffled, receding hair standing there but gave the identity up as a morphine mirage, it was so late. But the eyes, those green eyes, had unmistakably been there my entire life.

"Visiting hours are over," the figure began as he stepped into the room, "but that cute, little nurse let me back in since I'm your father."

His words came with a certain clarity that my ears had seldom heard. Moving to the chair beside the bed, he sat down quiet and dignified. He put his hand on my leg. Pain crept up my side but I didn't wince, this seemed too important.

"We're gonna be alright, you and me." He spoke directly to me. His words went into my ears and sent a spark into my brain, creating a shiver that ran throughout my entire body. And the only thing I could smell on his breath was honesty.

"Yea, Dad. I think we are."

There in the dark, we smiled at each other, perhaps the first we've ever shared together. Color me something I've never felt before.

Flash forward to the next afternoon when I started getting visitors. Word had circulated in my school about the accident and people flocked to my room: Kids that didn't like me, teachers that gave me bad grades and administrators that didn't "care for my attitude." Flowers, "Get Well" balloons and cute teddy bears began to grow around me like unchecked weeds in a garden.

Jonas Wellington, the second-string quarterback that had been bullying me for the past three years, wore melancholy on his face like a mask. He apologized for being such a huge prick to me—his words, not mine. I'm not sure if the apology was for me or for his old man, who I had heard was very tough with Jonas. He had been called down to the school on several occasions to deal with Jonas when he was caught pushing me around or threatening me. Mr. Wellington was an EMT and had been one of the first on scene at my accident. I quietly thanked him and accepted Jonas' apology and they were on their way.

Ms. Perkis, the 11th grade counselor who had told me that perhaps I should think about applying to a vocational school or joining the military instead of pursuing a four-year degree, dropped by a small wreath of flowers with a banner across it that said "Feel Better Soon" in bold, red-printed letters. She stayed for a few minutes, chit-chatting with my father about my progress this year and about what schools I was thinking about applying to later on. Her, with her smug recycled footwear and long flowing, bright yellow hippie skirt, telling me to come see her when I get back to school so that we can discuss my options for the future. This is an example of chaos as an instrument of creation—the possibilities of my bright future culminating from the clash of steel on steel and the death of my friends.

Victoria Sterling, Vicky to her friends and more importantly the girl that I had been in love with since the 5th grade, used a smile to hide the sadness from her frowns and make-up to hide the tears she had shed. I was confused because we hadn't spoken in a very long time—four or five years at least. Not since she blossomed into a beautiful swan, leaving me behind as an ugly duckling; also, she became a cheerleader. I suppose empathy hits some harder than others.

"I am so sorry about Carl and Dean and Joyce." The composure she was trying so hard to keep came crumbling down as she turned on the water works.

We hugged for a minute or two, her tears staining my hospital gown as she let loose into my shoulder.

"It's Okay, Vicky. It's Okay."

My words seemed hollow, even to me. It occurred to me that it was not Okay, but I didn't really want to think about it.

"Listen," she said as she drew away from me wiping her eyes, "When you get back on your feet, we should hang out, catch up." She smiled at me then. A smile I hadn't seen in a very long time. Her lips framed straight teeth that were a perfect shade of white and she showed them all when she smiled. "It's been too long." She wrote down her number on a sliver of paper and put on my bed side table, smiling all the while.

When she left she took my heart with her. I hoped to see it again soon. Color me craving.

Flash forward to earlier this morning, around three or so. An hour before, I had awakened from a nightmare about an unimaginably large snake curling around my entire body attempting to consume me slowly and methodically, enjoying every scream that came muffled from my mouth. A dream I've had since my mother died, intensified by morphine.

But now, in the eager twilight hours, I get half-hearted smiles and rushed greetings from third shift employees and nurses as I make my way up and down halls. Bored with walking my own floor, I take the elevator up two stories, to the

5th floor. I was wandering with no particular place to go but as long as you keep your head down, nobody will ask you any questions, not this early in the morning at least. I found myself on a ward where they kept people freshly released from the ICU—those well enough to be given their privacy, but still in need of watchful eyes.

I looked from side to side as I meandered down the hall, momentarily spying on those more misfortunate than myself, surprisingly grateful for my ability to walk for the first time. And then, with no signs or warning from the universe, there it was: Room 524 with its inhabitant Boyd, J. My mind felt put on pause and nothing was getting in or out. I looked down and saw an empty metal, folding chair right beside the door. No doubt a police detail, he was a criminal after all. But the policeman was nowhere to be found.

Entering the room with more than slight reservations from my legs, my heart was turned up to rapid-fire in my chest. Sweat appeared on my forehead, ignoring the cool air the air conditioning was creating. As I inched closer, almost close enough to see the man's face, I was startled almost into the air by a shrill ringing followed almost immediately by yelling and the quieted rushing of non-slip shoes. I turned to see what appeared to be two nurses and three orderlies rush by. They didn't notice me at all.

Turning back to the bed, I moved another four steps until I was standing over the man, peering down at this face. The moonlight created artificial light and menacing shadows over his face, which was varying shades of purple, blue and yellow, not to mention swollen. I had studied his picture in the paper, noting the lines and crevices and the eyes. They were dark hazel in the picture, but the eyes before me were shut, possibly swollen to the point where they couldn't open. The only aspect of him that was recognizable was his hair: That jet black hair that he wore back and ruffled that hung almost down to his shoulders.

"Josh, is that you?"

I asked the question knowing full well he would be unable to answer. He was undoubtedly on stronger drugs than I was and in a deep, hopefully terrifying, slumber. The moonlight revealed the handcuffs that kept him attached to the metal bed rails, there was my answer. He must've woken up, that's why he's on this ward. I imagine he gave quite a thrashing, not unlike my own response, to require the restraints. He was also sedated more than likely, unable to answer the questions the authorities must have for him. That's just as well. I didn't want him telling his secret.

My secret, our secret, was that he hadn't caused the collision. I had. I hadn't started out that evening with the intention of killing myself, the decision just crept over me through the course of the night. It was suppose to be a fun night for the four of us, which they usually were. Going out to get high on the old, stone bridge overlooking the town, Carl, Dean and Joyce were in exceptionally good moods. Mine was mediocre, but what else was new. Color me predictable.

I don't smoke weed, but for some reason that night, I really wanted to try it. After three hits my head was swimming in the clouds but drowning in a sea of sorrow at the same time— an over exaggerated version of my usual pity-party. If I didn't understand why my friends did this before, I really didn't get it then. But this is all just circumstance, the decision happened later and much faster.

Driving back into town we came upon a field that my mother used to take me to fly kites. I had three: One with dinosaurs, one with a drawing of Bat-man and the last was just a chaotic pattern of different colors. A memory of a day that we had went out to that field came to me like a wave of fleeting joy. There was nothing special about that day, it was just a sunny summer day. I remember the wind whipping across my face, helping ease the blaze from the sun. I had chosen my Bat-Man kite and he was flying high over me and my mother, his arms folded and his white eyes looking pointed and stern but I knew that he was there to protect us. To always keep us safe. After my mom died from leukemia, I threw that kite away, hating Bat-Man for his failure.

Driving, while trying to steady my head, I just listened to the conversations going on around me, going through me, leaving me behind. Carl blabbed on at a quickened pace about how he was planning to perform his routine at the next open-mike night held by our local 24-hour coffee shop. Dean, using his slow, cool method of speech, talked of his excitement for landing the role of Mercutio in the school's production of *Romeo and Juliet* that was starting rehearsal the next week. Joyce, quiet as ever, just laid her head on Dean's shoulder in the backseat, not saying a thing but we all knew that a million thoughts were racing through her head.

It was then, right then. A moment that would change everything forever. Right then, I knew that nothing mattered. Not having anything to say about anything that I was doing because I was doing nothing. This was it. I couldn't talk about future plans because no future existed for me. Not even an immediate one. I wanted it to end.

I didn't mean to hurt any of my friends, it all happened so quickly, as most of the results of bad decisions do. Coming to a four-way intersection, I eyed the truck to my left that was coming up fast to his stop sign. The truck was getting closer and closer to where it was suppose to stop and the driver was still not applying the brakes, the truck was not slowing down at all. It was going to run the stop sign. Carefully unbuckling my seat-belt so that no one would notice, I pushed the gear shift into first and held down the clutch pedal, waiting. As the bumper of the truck came into the intersection, I released the clutch and pressed down the accelerator with the full force of my foot, shooting us into the intersection. Steel crunched, metal folded back onto itself, bones broke, engines sputtered and died as the car rolled over and on its side. I didn't intend to wake up at all, but instead, I woke up free.

And at that moment—staring down into Josh Boyd's completely fucked up face—I knew that, now, I didn't want to die. The universe had shifted, the planets had realigned and I had found something I had long felt unattainable. I felt a sense of belonging, a sense of love and a lust for life. Holding on to my I.V. stand that always traveled with me for balance, I felt a sudden fear that locked my body and sent my mind reveling into an oblivion I no longer wanted to be in: I was afraid of losing what I had gained. Afraid of Josh Boyd waking up and telling the world that it hadn't been his fault; that I had ran through the stop sign, not him. Not that many people would believe a drunk driver reported of killing three teenagers, but I didn't feel like I could take that chance.

Standing there, gripping my I.V. stand, anger consumed fear and threw it by the wayside of my mind.

"You won't take this from me."

My eyes flashed red and I moved closer to his bed. I leaned over so that my mouth was right beside his ear.

"You hear me? You won't take this from me."

Color me vengeful.

I shuffled quickly back to the door and looked down the hall. The nurses and orderlies were still attending to another patient in another room. Moving back to the bed, I took another look at the man's face, contemplating another possible bad decision, but only for a moment. I shot my fist down hard into his chest, seizing his steady stream of breaths. As the upper half of his body curled upwards, I covered his mouth with my palm and forced him back down to his pillow. Leaving my I.V. stand, I took my other hand and clamped his nasal passages together, allowing no air flow.

A few seconds later, exasperated and quick breaths began hitting my palm followed by a low grumbling that could only be muffled screams trying to escape. And then, through a barricade of bruises, his eyes opened. Partially at first, they opened and he was looking up at me as I was looking down at him. But as bewilderment cascaded through those dark hazel eyes sunken into his sockets, his eyes widened and soon gave way to fear at the understanding that no air was leaving or entering his lungs. He tried to trash about but the handcuffs prevented him from helping himself. Looking up at me, the instrument of his destruction, he searched my face for some kind of recognition, something that would explain why this was happening. But I would give him no satisfaction. I felt his breath slow against my skin and watched his eyes roll towards the ceiling. I bent down to his ear again.

"Thank you."

Beep. Cough. Beep. And then I felt nothing.

THE DEBT COLLECTOR

Anson Rivers sat on his white plush couch sipping his 11:45 glass of Johnny Walker, just like most nights. Another smooth burning gulp from his glass, a slight yawn, and it was back to work. In front of his computer screen, Anson stared at the words on the page and pleaded with them to start working with one another to become great.

"Come on, you bastards," he whispered to himself in the dim light on the soundless television. "Come on."

The deadline was just a few weeks away and the publishers had already been sniffing around—phone calls, random visits and of course his wife would not leave him alone. He had been warned to not get involved with someone who worked for the company that he was technically employed by but Anson didn't care, he had fallen in love. At least for a spell.

Another soft sigh and Anson began running his fingers furiously across his keyboard, hitting key after key, typing word after word, looking for that magic something that landed him his publishing deal with the impressive Alias Publishing Co. over two years ago. So far, Anson had written two books and made a lot of money. Two out of five books he had been paid to write and the third one was now the biggest pain in the ass that Anson had ever experienced. After a weak two pages, he sat back against his couch and brought his glass to his lips another time.

A knock at the door stirred Anson from his daze. A look to the door to make sure that he wasn't hearing things and, after a second or two of waiting, three slow knocks followed the first. Anson raised his wrist to check his watch: The two hands said it was 11:59.

"What the fuck?" Anson uttered as he rose slowly up from the couch.

The walk over to the door seemed like it took forever. As Anson approached and reached for the handle, the black cat clock with the moving eyes on the wall beside the door struck midnight. Peering through the peep hole to get a look at the late night disturber Anson saw no one. The door handle felt ice cold in his palm as the door creaked open. No one was there. Anson blinked his eyes, wondering if he had imagined the sounds. A look to the left, a look to the right, and still no one in sight, but before he can close the door a gust of wind brushed past him. Anson stood bewildered in his doorway because there were no windows in the hallway.

"Hello, Mr. Rivers."

Anson turned to face the voice behind him. The man was several inches shorter than Anson and was dressed in shiny black loafers, sleek black slacks, a grey overcoat and a Rat Pack style hat pushed down as not to reveal his face. Anson, with his mouth gaping wide, backed away slowly only stopping when his back ran into the door. The door closed with the impact and the sound resonated throughout the silent apartment. Anson listened to his own shallow breaths and stared at the intruder. Everything about him was so alien and terrifying and yet, there was something strangely familiar.

"How did you get in here?" Anson finally asked.

"An irrelevant question, Mr. Rivers, the question you should be asking is…"

Anson pondered the intruder's statement, looking for the right question. "Why are you here?"

"There it is," the intruder said with a note of laughter in his voice. If Anson could see the face, he'd swear the man would be smiling. "I am here because of a debt."

"A debt?" Anson asked, back still against the door.

"Yes," the intruder said calm as a breeze, "a debt from a contract."

"You're here about my contract with Alias?" Anson could hear his own bewilderment.

"Do you think I am?" Again a note of laughter.

Anson watched as the intruder seemed to back away a few steps into his apartment without moving his feet and then a gust of what seemed like a black wind and the intruder was gone from view. Anson took a deep breath and exhaled slowly and shook his head from side to side. *What is happening to me?* He thought and rubbed his eyes. Then a noise from the living room moved Anson's feet quickly to investigate. The intruder was standing over his bar pouring a hearty glass of bourbon.

"Okay, what the hell is going on here?"

"Ah," the intruder said after taking a gulp and then let out a long sigh. "As I said, I'm here to collect on a debt."

"But I don't owe any debt," Anson said and moved to stand behind the couch because behind the couch was a small wooden table and on this table was a decorative wooden box and in this box was a .357 revolver. All Anson had to do was get the key ring from his pocket to unlock the box.

The intruder finished his bourbon with another big gulp and let out another long sigh. "Oh, but you do, son. But you do."

The intruder sat down the glass and walked to the middle of the room in front of the soundless television. Anson fiddled quietly with the keys in his pocket, withdrawing them without making any sound and running his fingers over each key looking for the right one.

"Did you know," the intruder began, his face still not visible, "that in certain instances, a verbal agreement is legally binding." He paused then, seemingly for effect. "But, then again, we're not dealing in legalities tonight."

Anson kept his eyes steady as he found the key and inserted slowly into the wooden box's lock. The intruder turned to the television and turned it off, leaving the only dim light in the room coming from Anson's still open computer screen. Anson had the box unlocked and lifted the lid soundlessly and put his hand around the handle of the revolver.

"You won't be needing that," the intruder said with his back still turned. He then faced Anson again, "what good would it do you anyway?"

Anson looked down for a second as he grasped the gun and brought it up level with the intruder, only the intruder was no longer there. Anson looked around the room quickly, pointing the gun everywhere his eyes went but seeing nothing out of the ordinary.

"What did you think was going to happen?" The intruder's voice came from nowhere.

Anson continued to stumble around the room, trying to follow the voice to its source. He made his way into the kitchen and turned on the light but still there was no one in sight. Anson walked back into the living room and looked around, trying to see anything. Another gust brushed against his face and suddenly the intruder is in front of him and the gun is gone from his hand before Anson can even let out a breath.

"I was hoping," the intruder said as he backed away a few feet, "that this would be civil."

"What are you?"

"Not what am I, Mr. Rivers, but *why* am I."

Anson couldn't understand. "Why are you?" It made no sense.

"You really don't remember?" The question sounded playful and Anson imagined another chuckle. "You created me—well, the way I look anyway."

Anson stared at the intruder with wide eyes. He looked at the shiny black shoes and the memory invaded his consciousness instantly: A short story he had written almost ten years ago and the character that had come to him in a dream. The black shoes, the sleek black pants, the overcoat tied tight across the body and the hat that never let you see the face. Anson felt the air in his lungs congeal and his heart stop.

"Now, I know what you're thinking," the intruder began, "but I'm not 'the devil.'" His gloved hands rose to produce air quotes.

Anson's heart restarted and he could breathe again. "Then what are you?" He asked the intruder quietly.

"An agent."

"Or a servant?" Anson muttered defiantly.

"Yes," the intruder said after a pause, "you could say that."

"So, if you're not the devil then why do you look like that?"

"To help you better understand the situation." The intruder moved back a few steps and motioned towards the couch. "Please, sit." Anson looked to the couch but didn't attempt to move his body. A low rumble filled his ears. "I said sit!"

The intruder seemed to roar and Anson thought the walls might be shaking. Without thought or conscious movement Anson made his way to the couch and sat down, his eyes never leaving the *thing* he had created.

"Thank you," the intruder said in a polite, calm voice. "Now, do you remember the plot to your story?"

Anson closed his eyes and went over many years and hundreds of thousands of words to a short story that he hadn't thought of in a very long time. He opened his eyes. "It was about the devil coming to collect on a deal he had made with a man in order to make him very wealthy."

"And what did the devil come to collect?" Anson thought he could hear glee in the intruder's voice.

After a moment of thought, Anson answered, "That which the man valued most."

"And with all of this man's wealth and fame and possessions, what did the devil take?"

Anson gulped and felt the weight of a rock in his throat. "His life," he said almost silently, "the man valued his life the most."

"Exactly."

The intruded leaned over just enough for Anson to see into the blackness under his hat and what he saw sent chills throughout his being. Glowing green orbs for eyes, not red like everyone would think, but green. The darkest green one can imagine but with a glow resonating from them. The eyes that Anson had given to him. And in them he saw the evil that he had created.

"But I've made no deal," Anson said, suddenly frantic, "I think I would remember making a deal with the goddamn devil."

"God-damned indeed," the intruder stood straight up again, "but perhaps you need some help remembering."

The intruder walked slowly around the coffee table, the dim light from the open lap top illuminating his every step. Anson wanted to get up and run, try to flee, but he knew that it would do him no good. With the intruder in front of him, Anson stared straight down at the floor, anticipating what was going to happen. The intruder raised his gloved hand and put it lightly onto Anson's head. A coldness that Anson had never felt before swept over him and then he was plunged into darkness. When the light returned Anson blinked and saw himself sitting at a shabby desk in front of a computer screen with his face buried in his hands. They were in a crappy, dimly lit apartment that was painted sea foam green.

"What is this?" Anson said, looking around the room.

"This is you," the intruder said standing beside him, "in your finest moment."

The Anson sitting at the desk raised his head from his hands—visible streaks were on his cheeks from where he had been crying. He stared at the computer screen, stared through it to the words on it and their meaning.

"Why won't you work?" He bellowed at the screen and then shook it violently.

"My first book attempt," the Anson in the corner of the room whispered, "four years ago."

The Anson sitting at the desk put his face back into his hands and proceeded to weep. The Anson in the corner wanted to go over to his former self and put a reassuring hand on his shoulder. He wanted to tell him that everything would be okay, that he was going to make everything work. He began to move but the intruder put his hand on Anson's shoulder and his hat shook in a 'no' fashion.

"Ah!" The Anson at the desk suddenly bellowed into the air and pounded clenched fists furiously against the desk. He then stood up and hurled a notebook against a wall. It bounced off and landed on the floor with a thud. He paced back and forth, muttering and shaking his head. And then, looking at the notebook on the floor, he took a few steps and knelt beside it.

"God," the Anson on the floor began and then raised his head, "please, I'll do anything if you will just help me out here. I've put everything I have into this. Please, I need help," And then lowered his head once more.

Anson's eyes went wide. He shook off the intruder's hand and ran over to his former self. "What are you doing, you damned fool?" He screamed into his ear. "You can do this on your own! I've already done it!" But the Anson sitting at the desk did not hear him. "I've already done it," he whispered as everything darkened again.

When the light returned Anson was back sitting on the couch in his new, expensive apartment and he gasped for air. The intruder removed his hand from Anson and moved back to standing behind the coffee table. Anson inhaled a deep breath and exhaled slowly to calm his heart.

"God wasn't listening that day," the intruder said, humor once again on his tongue, "but someone else was." Anson just stared straight ahead, not knowing what to say. "What, did you really think that it came to you on your own? That the heavens just opened up and gave you the words?" A low laugh emanated from the intruder but to Anson it sounded more like a jackal.

"So you're here for my life?"

The intruder's hat cocked to the side. "Goodness no, I'm here for what you value most, Mr. Rivers."

"If not for my life then what?" Anson stared into the darkness trying to see the green orbs. "What possible need could you have for money?"

"None," the intruder answered quickly and calmly.

"Then what…" Anson's eyes went wide with fear.

Another low jackal laugh and the intruder vanished into his dark essence and moved with a gust. Anson jumped up from the couch, knocked the coffee table over and spilling his laptop onto the floor. Running down the hall, his mind racing, Anson almost tripped over his own feet. Finally he is at the last door on the right and, as he rushes into the room, he sees the intruder looming over the side of his four month old son's crib, the street light outside the window illuminating his silhouette. Anson freezes and the room is deathly silent.

"He really is a beautiful child," the intruder's voice rips through the air.

"Don't you touch him, you bastard."

"You're not really in a position to be making demands," the intruder said in a low but stern tone as he reached down towards the baby, "Mr. Rivers."

Anson took two steps and lunged towards the intruder, not surprisingly hitting nothing until he crashed into the wall beside the crib. Anson sat up slowly, leaning his back against the wall and feeling the fire that burned in his left shoulder and ran all the way down his arm and sizzled in his finger tips.

"How long are we going to play these games, Mr. Rivers?" The intruder had reappeared in front of the crib and was still looking down at the baby. "You sooner you understand how powerless you are, the sooner this will all be over."

Anson tried to stand but as he was pulling himself up the wall the intruder raised a gloved hand and pointed at the ground with his index finger and Anson was suddenly, and forcibly, back on the ground.

"You can't do this," Anson panted through excruciating breaths, "you can't do this."

"Can't I?" The intruder said with a low, angry tone which immediately became a deafening roar, "Can't I?!" And then the intruder reached down into the crib again.

Anson struggled to get up with all the strength in his body and, after failing miserably, collapsed against the wall. "Please," he pleaded with what air remained in his lungs, "I beg you, don't do this."

"The time for begging is over, Mr. Rivers. You have to learn that you can't have everything you want without a price." The hat turned in Anson's direction and the green orbs shined with the fire of eternity in the darkness. "This is your lesson."

Freezing wind filled the room as the intruder touched the boy and seemed to consume Anson's essence as he again struggled to get up. His lungs felt like they were melting and bones wanted to break but Anson continued his quest to stand. After what seemed like forever but also like no time had passed at all, the wind stopped and Anson once again collapsed against the wall, feeling lifeless. The intruder's hand was once again at his side and he let out a long and accomplished sigh.

"Thank you for your cooperation, Mr. Rivers," the intruder said as he turned around and moved towards the door, "it won't be forgotten." And then he was gone.

Anson, once again left to his own will, stood feebly, placed his hands on the side of the crib and peered in. What he saw was his son lying there, wrapped in a robin's egg blue blanket, but not in a way Anson had ever seen him before. He was not giggling or gurgling or crying or cooing. He just lied there, silent and still, with his fragile head turned to the side and his penetrating brown eyes staring into nothingness. Anson would cry, if he had anything left in him but as it turns out, there was nothing.

"Brian," Anson mutters and ruffles his son's thin black hair, the boy still not moving.

With weak arms Anson lifted his son out of the crib, blanket and all, and cradled him against his still burning shoulder. The walk down the hall and into the living room happened in slow motion and Anson felt much older than he was as he sidestepped the overturned coffee table and sat on his plush white couch. Anson looked to the watch on his wrist: the two hands said it was 12:37 in the morning. Hannah would be back from her girl's night out soon. With his son against his shoulder Anson wondered what he was going to tell his wife. *What would she believe? What would anyone believe?*

The truth was too horrible for words.

GIFT

Part One: A Helping Hand

Abigail Sawyer sits upright in her hospital bed staring into the eyes of her ragged stuffed dog with one ear which she had happily named "Scraps." Scraps has been with Abigail almost as long as she's been alive, or so her mother says; and now, it will outlive her. The tragedy is not lost on nine year old Abigail.

Months have passed since the chemo-therapy stopped yielding results for Abigail's tiny, withered body. Her scalp begins to itch but she won't even bother to remove the mess of shoulder length blonde hair that rests on her head to scratch it. Abigail had chosen that particular wig because it reminded her of her mother's hair.

After Abigail collapsed in her house two days ago, her doctor said the news was grim—she had a few days left, a week at best. But Abigail knew better. Her parents, whom had barely left her side, were crumbling under the weight of what was coming and have currently stepped out of the room for a bite to eat. Abigail is using her precious alone time to say good-bye to Scraps. Holding the dog in her hands—looking deep into its dark marble eyes—Abigail feels...well, she feels nothing. She's been dying almost as long as she's been living: The tears have been shed, her good-byes have been said and her time is almost up. The only thing that she does feel currently is the desire to feel anything else. And, suddenly, she does.

The barely visible blonde hairs on Abigail's arms stand on end. Her face flushes with heat and the breath almost leaves her body. Looking up from Scraps, she sees a man standing casually in the doorway. He is wearing black shoes, dark blue denim jeans and a black long sleeve shirt with a candy cane colored vest over it. Black gloves are on his hands. His short brown hair is ruffled and his face says that he hasn't shaved in days.

"You don't look like a volunteer," Abigail's words come quietly out of her and she clutches Scraps to her chest.

"Well, I am," the stranger says with a low but oddly soothing voice. "Of sorts."

The stranger walks slowly over to the bed and sits on the edge beside Abigail's feet. The call button for the nurse lies on the bed inches from Abigail's fingers but she doesn't reach for it, she doesn't feel like she has to. The stranger's face says he's still a young man but his eyes say he's tired, and very old. The lights dim in the room behind his head—this might be her eyes deceiving her or something far more evil but, to Abigail, it feels strangely calming but not without traces of fear.

"Why are you here?" She asks, trying to show her bravery but clutching Scraps tighter than ever.

A faint smile crosses the stranger's face and then disappears like it never happened. "To give you what you want."

The stranger takes off the glove on his left hand and places his fingers on Abigail's shin: The room shakes and crumbles away, by pieces at first, and then the darkness swallows them both. It is cold and empty and to Abigail seems vast and eternal. Then light begins to break through, slowly at first, rising somewhere from the endless night until it consumes everything. It is blinding beyond comprehension and there is warmth.

The stranger removes his fingers from Abigail's leg: The hospital room comes back and it's just as it had been. Abigail touches her face to make sure that she, and everything else, is real. Looking at the stranger—that faint smile back on his face—she turns to her mother's Bible on the night stand and then back to the stranger. His smile has disappeared once more.

"Are you an angel?"

He chuckles. "No, kid, I'm no angel."

Abigail looks the stranger over with widened eyes and comes to rest on the name tag on his candy cane vest. Pointing to it she says, "But your name is Gabriel."

There is no chuckle this time. "Don't let that fool you, kid."

Abigail stares into the stranger's eyes: The blue makes her think of an ocean she's only seen once in her life. She had been scared then—looking over the edge of the boat into a deep, dark blue that she couldn't even fathom where the bottom was while her parents took pictures of fish. Thinking about it now, Abigail wasn't scared, but relieved. "How did you find me?"

"Did you feel me?"

Gabriel's words cascaded over her and Abigail remembered the sudden heat in her cheeks and the chill that had went up her spine. Abigail nods.

"Well, I felt you, too," he inches closer to her. "Are you ready?" Abigail nods again. "Give me your hand."

Still holding Scraps with her right arm, Abigail extends her left hand into Gabriel's open palm. It stays this way for a few seconds. Abigail flashes a weary smile while a tear crawls from the corner of her eye. Gabriel clamps his hand around hers and the darkness returns.

Gabriel sits on the bed, holding Abigail's hand, waiting for her machines to stop beeping.

Part Two: Redemption Seeker

Gabriel had already spent most of the day, as he spends most of everyday, walking around St. Luke's getting patients their medications, retrieving files for doctors and making coffee for nurses. Gabriel works more hours than any other volunteer in the hospital, barely taking any breaks and sometimes only leaving when someone in charge tells him it's time to go. The staff speculated as to how the twenty-two year old was able to be there all the time as a volunteer who wasn't making any money. They arrived at the theory that he must be that rare breed of rich kid that wants to work and give something back so he lives off of a trust fund and lends the majority of his time to the hospital. This theory is mostly correct except for the fact that he lives off of an inheritance, not a trust fund. And, also, it is his guilt that drives Gabriel. Not his kindness.

Currently, Gabriel is walking through the Sullivan Wing of St. Luke's—it's the wing for geriatrics. The day has been routine so far: Checking on patients, getting meds and playing checkers with Mrs. Ross for half an hour. But now, walking to the bathroom, Gabriel is seized by that old, familiar feeling. A cold sweat begins to build on his palms underneath his gloves as a shiver that Gabriel's body can barely weather immediately follows. He drops to one knee, attempting to catch his breath and lower his heart rate. Gasping for air, Gabriel knows what has to happen.

"Oh, my Lord, honey, are you okay?" Gabriel looks up as Patricia, the fifty-something year old nurse who's on the edge of retirement, bumbles towards him in her pink scrubs.

"Yea, I'm fine," he mutters as she pulls him up by his arm to help steady him as he stands.

"Well, are you sure?" She is genuinely concerned.

"Yea, I'm good." He gives her a reassuring smile but she still eyes him as she walks away down the hall.

Gabriel is used to this. Three times out of five somebody witnesses his body's reaction to the sudden knowledge that he is going to take a life. He looks to his left and then to his right at the rooms trying to figure out what has changed: There is no one in the room to his left so it must be Mr. Miller to his right.

Clyde Miller is eighty-two years old and had been admitted a couple of weeks ago for heart failure. Gabriel had sat and chatted with the man on a few occasions and he hadn't gotten the impression that the man wanted to die. Regardless, Gabriel enters the room slowly to a steady beep of monitors and long, drawn breaths from Mr. Miller with the help of his oxygen machine. The hairs on Gabriel's arms and neck stand on end and a dull throb enters his temples and his chest begins to ache; this is where he's supposed to be.

"Mr. Miller?" Gabriel speaks softly, the man looks somewhere between life and death but then flickers his eyes opens and focuses them.

He removes the oxygen mask from his nose and mouth. "Gabe? Is that you?"

"Yes, Sir." Mr. Miller had been a Sergeant in the army and liked to be called "Sir."

"I'm just checking up on you, seeing how you're doing today." Gabriel forces a smile.

Mr. Miller blinks a few times. "Oh, well…that's nice of you."

The silence is awkward. Gabriel is always unsure of how to broach the subject of "I can end your life" with someone who already knows who he is. Maybe that's because he doesn't like the contrast of the "nice guy" persona he portrays with someone only to have them suddenly view him as the harbinger of death.

"Is there anything I can help you with today?" The question is out there and Gabriel hopes Mr. Miller will take the cue.

"Oh, no, that's alright, son," he takes a drag from his oxygen mask and removes it again. "I'm feeling okay."

Liar, thinks Gabriel. *Just make this easier and admit it.*

Mr. Miller momentarily turns his head to his night stand, blinks and then turns back. The only thing on the night stand is the phone. Gabriel can see the desire of death in the old man's eyes, now. They have lost that spark, that *living* essence that was there only a day or two ago.

"Are you waiting on a phone call, Sir?"

"No," he says, taking a deep breath and closing his eyes. "I already got one this morning." Gabriel stands by the foot of the bed, waiting for Mr. Miller to say what his eyes were trying to. After a long pause he says, "My wife died." Tears form at the corners of his eyes and flow down his cheeks.

A lump rises in Gabriel's throat with understanding, he's been here before. He sits on the edge of the bed. "How did it happen?" The words barely make their way out.

Mr. Miller takes another long drag from his mask, seemingly more to gain his composure than the actual need for oxygen. He wipes the corners of his eyes before he speaks. "She fell." More tears start to form. "She fell getting out of the tub and hit her head."

Gabriel lets the words hang in the air knowing that there is nothing he can say or do—not even the gift of death—that will help at this moment. Remembering being completely helpless and alone, Gabriel's heart begins to beat faster and his chest begins to ache. Some wounds never do truly close.

"She was so strong for me," Mr. Miller began with a new hint of anger in his voice. "She was so strong and so loving and

I promised I'd be strong for her." He is no longer trying to hide his tears as he speaks. "I know, not think, *know* that the only reason I've held on this long is sheer determination. I've never failed at anything I've set my mind to. And now…" Mr. Miller trails off and stares at the ceiling, not bothering to wipe his eyes.

Gabriel lets all of this settle before he speaks. "Mr. Miller…"

"It should've been me, Goddamnit," he interrupts in an explosion, "she didn't deserve to die, she still had so much life left." He needs oxygen from the outburst. "It should've been me," he grumbles lowly to himself after removing his mask again.

Gabriel takes off the glove on his right hand and scoots closer. "Mr. Miller, I have something for you."

Mr. Miller chuckles and then coughs softly. "I was wondering when you were gonna get to that."

"Sir?" Gabriel hears the bewilderment in his own voice.

"What? You think I don't know what you are?" There is a strange smile on the old man's face. "I fought and survived a war, son, I know that look in a man's eyes: The sorrow and the hatred. You're looking for understanding. A way to make it right." He pauses to inspect Gabriel's face, "I had you pegged the moment I saw you."

Gabriel, in shock, begins to put his glove back on his hand not knowing what to do next. This dying old man couldn't possibly know what he is—Gabriel didn't even understand it himself. Before he can get the glove all the way on his hand, Mr. Miller reaches out and lightly grabs Gabriel's wrist. Looking up into the old man's face is all the permission he needs. Gabriel removes his glove once more.

"One favor?" The anger has left Mr. Miller's voice and his smile has faded. "Make it peaceful?"

"It's not what you think it is," is all Gabriel can say.

81

Mr. Miller lies back onto his bed and looks up at the ceiling. Gabriel takes the old man's hand, squeezes it with his own and closes his eyes. The room begins to shake, something that Gabriel has never experienced. Opening his eyes with panic, Gabriel sees the same panic in the old man's. Then the darkness comes, slowly at first, and then covering everything that Gabriel sees. There is fear and cold in the dark, a cold like he has never felt before and Gabriel feels his heart beating so hard against his chest that he thinks it might explode. Quickly releasing Mr. Miller's hand, Gabriel falls to floor and feels the harshness of linoleum against his head. From above him, Gabriel hears painful and terrified gasps.

"It's not supposed to be like this," Gabriel mutters, his mouth against the floor. "It's not supposed to be like this." And then everything is black.

Part Three: Penance and Atonement

Kristen watches the stranger sleep. He had been brought into the room, unconscious, an hour ago. Since his arrival he has periodically murmured to himself, twitched and turned his head back and forth. Kristen hasn't been able to make sense of his murmurs but has noticed that the stranger seems distressed. Looking at him—with his gruff face and ruffled hair—he looks older than he is. Kristen guesses that he's in his early twenties.

When she had passed by the room shortly after the doctors had left, Kristen had felt that old, familiar feeling. But now, sitting here beside him, she does not know what to feel. Especially since she had laid her hand on him and nothing had happened—something she has never experienced. To say that Kristen is curious about this stranger is putting it lightly. So, now she waits for him to wake up so they can have a chat.

The stranger's eyes flutter and he exhales deeply. Looking only at the ceiling at first, he takes another deep breath, wincing in pain, and then—noticing Kristen out of the corner of his eye—the stranger tilts his head to meet her gaze.

"Hello," Kristen says in her ever-practiced sweet voice and flashes her pearly whites.

The stranger rubs his eyes for a second and looks at her, probably trying to make sure she isn't a hallucination. "Hello." His voice is low and rough but strangely soothing.

"I'm Kristen."

"Gabriel," he offers with a faint smile. His eyes remind Kristen of the ocean.

"Like the angel?"

Gabriel gives a little chuckle and looks at his feet sticking out from the covers. "Yeah, like the angel."

Kristen watches his eyes dart around the room and then come to settle on the I.V. needle in his forearm and then his hands. He stares at his skin as if he expects something else to be there and then sighs. As he looks up, Kristen sees wonderment in Gabriel's eyes as he studies her hospital gown and I.V. that match his own. "You're dying." Kristen recognizes this as a statement, not a question.

"That obvious, huh?" Kristen says this with a grin and a half-hearted laugh to mask her pain.

Gabriel closes his eyes, draws in a deep breath and exhales slowly opening his eyes again. "But you don't want to die."

Again, Kristen hears a statement and not a question. Bewildered, she doesn't know really know what to say to that. "Um…no, I don't," she offers a confused smile and another half-hearted laugh. "Nobody does."

"You'd be surprised." Gabriel's voice is low and definitive. Kristen doesn't hear pessimism, she hears knowledge, and is frightened by the prospect. Looking her way again, he gingerly asks, "So, what's wrong with you?"

Kristen stares into his eyes trying to watch the waves rocking back and forth but, instead, only sees curiosity in them. "I have a clot in my brain and the doctors don't know why." She looks down at her hands. "But I know that it's going to aneurysm and it's going to bleed into my brain and I'm going to die."

The matter-of-fact way that Kristen says this must have caught Gabriel off guard because he sits all the way up in his bed and intensifies his stare at her. "How do you know that?"

Kristen thinks for a second. "Because I feel it," was the best way that she could explain how she knew what was going to happen. It's how she always knew what was going to happen to people.

"You feel it?" The curiosity in his eyes disappears but is replaced by something else, something Kristen can't quite put her finger on. Gabriel looks down at his hands again and then back at Kristen.

"Are you okay?" It's all that Kristen can think to say.

"No, not really."

"So, what's wrong with *you*? I'm pretty good at spotting what's wrong with people but with you...I have no idea." Kristen says while smiling, trying to lighten the mood a little.

"What? Besides the obvious?" Gabriel smiles and touches his bandaged head with his fingers only to recoil slightly in pain. Kristen stares at him, waiting for the answer. He sighs. "Lung cancer."

"Funny, I wouldn't have pegged you for a smoker."

"I'm not," he gives a light smile. "But that's the way the dice land."

Kristen is bumbling around thoughts in her hand on how to broach the subject of her touch earlier when they are interrupted by a knock at the door. Julie, a nurse on their floor that Kristen has spoken to a few times, stands in the door frame: Long dark hair up, stethoscope around her neck and holding a chart, as usual.

"Hey, Julie." Gabriel says. The casualness of his tone intrigues Kristen. *So he's familiar with the staff.* She ponders this while the two speak.

"Hey, Gabe, how are you feeling?"

"I'm alive." Gabriel says this with little enthusiasm.

"Well, that's the important thing," she looks at the chart in her hands briefly. "I'll go tell Dr. Jensen you're awake."

Julie begins to walk away but Gabriel stops her: "What happened to Mr. Miller?" The concern in his voice spikes. This, too, interests Kristen very much.

Julie makes a solemn face and walks two steps into the room. "He's in a coma," she lets that settle for a moment. "Looks like he lapsed into it about the time we found you on the floor." She offers a small, courteous smile and is then out the door. Gabriel again stares at his hands.

"Is he related to you?" Kristen asks to break the silence.

"No," Gabriel says, his voice cracking a bit. "I had just talked to him a few times."

"Do you work here?" She needs to regain his attention.

He shakes his head back and forth slightly. "Volunteer."

"Well, that's very noble of you, Gabriel."

He turns slowly, his eyes reddening as if he's fighting back tears. "No, it's not, it's a petty attempt…" he breaks off and stares out the door. "And I'm here and I can't even help…" The tears start to come then and he buries his head in his hands.

"Help who? What are you attempting to do?" She reaches to put her hand on Gabriel's arm to get him to look at her but he jerks away from her violently and almost falls off the other side of his bed.

"Don't," is all he says as he stares at Kristen. He reminds her of a frightened animal. "You can't," he says softly.

"Why can't I?" She inches her chair until it's right beside the bed.

"I don't want anything else bad to happen."

"Anything else?"

"I was just trying to help him," the tears return to his eyes. "He just wanted to go."

"Who wanted to go where?"

Gabriel lowers his head and begins to sob softly, his shoulders shaking with every sniffle. Kristen will let him have his grief but first they have to talk. She grabs him by the shoulders and shakes him. He looks at her and then at then her hands on his shoulders. "You see? Nothing bad is going to happen." He continues to stare at her. "But I have to tell you something."

Gabriel sits cross-legged at the head of the bed; Kristen sits on the foot of the bed and mimics him. She takes a deep breath before beginning.

"When I was little, I discovered that I could…" she thinks for a moment before continuing, "heal people." Her words sit heavy in the air and she waits for Gabriel to respond.

"Heal people?" He asks with a straight face.

"Yes, but only people who weren't going to get better on their own. Do you know what I mean?" She realizes the question is dumb, of course he doesn't know what she means. He just continues to stare. "Well, anyway, I was walking by the room and I felt you in pain. A pain you can't handle yourself." Kristen waits a moment to gather her thoughts and is about to continue when Gabriel interrupts her.

"How did you feel it?"

"Excuse me?"

"You said you felt my pain," he turns and looks into Kristen's eyes, "how?"

"Oh..." Kristen had never been asked to explain it before. "Well, it's like a throbbing in my head, or more like a vibration, really. That's actually how they found the clot. It's been with me for as long as I can remember. A few years ago I discovered that the vibrations happen when I'm near someone who needs help."

"And you think I need help?"

"I don't think," Kristen points to her head and smiles. "I know."

Gabriel smiles, nods his head and looks down at his hands. "Of course."

"So, anyway, I came in and you were unconscious and I thought this would be better 'cause I wouldn't have to explain anything so I put my hand on your arm and nothing happened. I mean, literally, nothing. You didn't even wake up. That's never happened to me before. So, of course, you can see that I was naturally curious about how this could have happened so I sat down to wait for you to wake up and...here we are."

Gabriel blinks a few times. "You talk a lot don't you?"

Kristen smiles and looks away, slightly embarrassed. "When I'm nervous or excited."

"So, which is it?

Kristen takes the question into account. "A little bit of both, I guess."

"Well, don't be. It's not a problem with you." Kristen watches his face, waiting for an explanation. "It's me."

"What do you mean?"

"I don't deserve to be healed," Gabriel looks up at her, his eyes lost in his own memories. "I've done terrible things."

"Like what?" Kristen replies with a laugh and smile, thinking maybe he is joking.

"We're opposites—you give life while I only give," Gabriel eyes move slowly down to stare at his hands in his lap, "death."

Kristen joins Gabriel in staring at his hands, she couldn't believe it. There is someone else like her. She hurriedly wraps her arms around his neck and hugs him tight.

"I've been alone for so long." Kristen feels her eyes begin to mist.

Gabriel wrenches her arms away from his neck and stares deep into her eyes. Kristen can't help but smile even at Gabriel's scowl. "How can you be happy about this?"

"How can you not be?" Kristen is bewildered at his response. "We're not alone—it's not just you or me."

"I kill people!" Gabriel exclaims and then shrinks back down into himself, looking ashamed. "I am alone."

Kristen thinks about what could possibly be the right thing to say in this situation but comes up with nothing. "When did it first happen?" She asks to keep him talking.

Gabriel sniffs and rubs his eyes. "It's been happening as long as I've been alive, or at least, for as long as I can remember anyway." Kristen places her hand gently on his knee, expecting him to move it away but, surprisingly, he doesn't. "I think it was sporadic, at first," Gabriel continues, still looking down. "We had pets when I was young, and everything was fine for awhile but it always ended the same—they would suddenly die when I was petting or holding them. By the time I was six my parents said no more and I was basically left on my own. They were too busy taking care of my older brother to have time for me. He had a rare blood disease and had been dying for a long time. My parents spent virtually every dollar we had to try to just give him a little more time.

88

Kristen watches Gabriel fighting back his tears and starts to feel some of her own but she always lets herself cry. "I'm so sorry, Gabriel. I can only imagine how hard that must've been."

Finally crying, Gabriel starts to chuckle and that turns into a laughing fit. "The funny thing is," he says through tears and giggles before regaining some composure, "Mikey didn't want to live…he just wanted the suffering to be over—his and our parents." Gabriel looks up in Kristen's eyes but she can tell that he's looking somewhere else, maybe into the past. "He knew what I was before I did."

"How?" Kristen asks, mesmerized by every word that he's saying.

"I don't know," he blinks his eyes and Kristen sees him looking at her now. "But one Saturday morning I woke up early and was going downstairs to get some cereal. When I walked by Mikey's room I got this sudden chill like I had never felt before. It knocked me to my knees and then my head started to pound and my chest felt like it was going to explode."

Kristen inches closer to Gabriel on the bed until their knees are touching. If he notices he makes no indication.

"I was trying to catch my breath when Mikey called my name. It was real casual, like nothing was wrong, just 'Gabriel, come here.' So, I went in and there he was in his bed, like always, staring at me with those sunken, hollow eyes. I remember he was so pale, like a piece of chalk that could talk to you." Gabriel breaks his concentration and looks around the room, almost as if he had forgotten where he is.

"What happened?" Kristen realizes that the enthusiasm for hearing the story is inappropriate and tries to put on an apologetic expression.

"He just looked at me and said 'it's time,'" Gabriel says, staring at the wall behind Kristen. "'I'm ready.'"

"What did you do?"

"I didn't know what to do, or what he meant. He scared me shitless, actually." Gabriel turns his head back to look at Kristen. "I just stood there, silent. But he knew: He reached out and took my hand with both of his. It looked like it took all he had in him to do that. And, I'll never forget, he said 'Let go. Just let me go.' I squeezed his hand because I was scared and... and then he was gone."

Tears fall from the corners of his eyes freely now as he stares into Kristen's eyes. Kristen feels hers start to do the same and she reaches out and hugs Gabriel tight, maybe tighter than she's ever hugged anyone. "Gabriel, you can't blame yourself for that. It sounds like you did something wonderful for your brother."

Gabriel breaks away from the hug while still holding Kristen by the shoulders. The pain just keeps growing in his eyes. "I know," he says with utter conviction, "I know I did right by my brother. It's what...it's what happened next that I..."

Kristen watches as his eyes seem to dim and grow a darker blue and he begins to breathe quicker, like he's grasping for air. "What happened, Gabriel?"

"I...I killed them," he mutters, almost inaudibly. "I killed them."

"Killed who?"

"My parents," Gabriel says as he releases Kristen and sits back against his pillow. "I killed my parents. I've never told anyone that before."

"What happened?" Kristen asks in a low voice, hoping not to upset him.

Gabriel's eyes shake with his hands as he again stares into nothing. "Mom and dad came in just after it happened, I was still holding Mikey's hand. My dad saw Mikey first, could see that he was dead, and he backhanded me. I don't know why he was so angry—I don't think he knew what I could do. I cowered in the corner while mom hugged Mikey and started bawling her eyes out. Dad tried to comfort her but it was no use."

Gabriel starts to say something but closes his mouth and just lets his lips quiver with the memory. "It's okay," Kristen again touches his hand lightly with her fingers. "You can tell me."

He looks down at her hand resting on his and sniffles. "After a minute, Dad stopped trying to comfort mom and came toward me," Gabriel looks up into Kristen's eyes. "He grabbed me by the shoulders—I can still see the anger in his eyes. All he said was 'you little bastard. What did you do?' I tried to explain that Mikey had asked for my help, that he just wanted to go, but it was too late. Dad was shaking me and I put my hands on his arms. I just wanted him to stop."

Gabriel starts to wipe away the tears with the back of his hand. Being rather unsuccessful, Kristen hands him a tissue from the box on the nightstand. "Go on," she urges with a friendly tone.

Gabriel blows his nose softly and composes himself. "He started to gasp for air and that's when mom came over. She pulled him away but it was too late—I watched him die on the floor. Mom came at me then. I just put my hand up to try and keep her away but she grabbed it and slapped me with her free hand. She never let go of me, though. By the time I recovered from the slap, she was already about to collapse."

Gabriel turns his head away and blows his nose again. Kristen is letting everything he just told her sink in, unsure of what to say. After a second, she carefully says, "It wasn't your fault."

Gabriel looks back at her, astonishment covering his face. "How can you say that? Of, course it's my fault," he exclaims. "Death is in my hands and *they* killed my family—my hands!"

Kristen lets silence blanket the room because she knows there is nothing constructive that can be said. "So, what happened next?" She asks after a minute, just to keep Gabriel talking.

"The doctors and the police couldn't figure out what had happened," he says, his calm, low voice returning. "I was only nine years old but that didn't keep me out of suspicion. I was put in a detention center for a week but when they went over every inch of our lives, and our house, they determined that there was no *physical* evidence that said I did anything so they let me go. Needless to say, I started wearing gloves whenever I was around anyone else."

"Where did you go?"

"To live with my Great Uncle Gerald; he was fifty-nine at the time but my only living relative and had the means to support me. We basically just politely stayed out of each other's way. I think he was scared of me. He died when I was seventeen."

Kristen arches one of her eyebrows to give Gabriel a mockingly suspicious look. He smiles back at her. "No, I had nothing to do with that." He chuckles to himself and then resets his face. "He had a heart attack."

"So, you've been on your own ever since?"

"Pretty much. I had to go to a foster home for a few months but then I turned eighteen, got my inheritance and split. He left me a good amount of his money 'cause he didn't have any other family either."

"And, what, you've been working at hospitals ever since helping people die?" Kristen asks with a smile.

"You joke, but that's about right." Gabriel's face stays serious. "I spent awhile thinking of how to redeem myself, to try and atone for what I had done. I decided I would help people," tears return to his eyes, "like I helped Mikey."

"But how can you tell who needs help?"

"I feel it," Gabriel says in a very matter-of-fact way. "Just like you do. The exact same way I felt it with Mikey," he takes in a deep breath, "every time."

"Is that what you were doing when you feel and hit your head?"

Gabriel looks into Kristen's eyes with a certain sadness on his face but it doesn't seem to be for himself. "Mr. Miller just wanted to go be with his wife; I just wanted to help him but I fucked it up."

"What happened with him?"

"I have no idea. Everything was going the same as it always does and then…" Gabriel trails off and looks away, "everything just went black and it was cold, so cold. And it felt like it was forever, like there was no escaping it." He blinks and refocuses on Kristen. "I remember pulling my hand away, I guess that's when I fell and hit my head." He sniffles once again. "I think that's why he's in a coma—I pulled away before it was over."

"You can't blame yourself for that," Kristen says suddenly. Gabriel looks confused. "You don't know what would have happened if you had held onto him. You might've died, too."

"Yeah, well, I think the world would've been all right with that."

Kristen grabs Gabriel by the shoulders and shakes him. "You. Cannot. Blame. Yourself. Yes, you've been through a lot of shit but you were a little kid who didn't know any better. How many people have you helped since then?"

Gabriel is taken aback by Kristen's outburst. "I dunno, a couple dozen, maybe…"

"You see?" Kristen interrupts, "You were put here for a reason. You were given this *gift* for a reason." A smile widens on Kristen's face.

"It's not a gift," is all that Gabriel says.

"I know you don't see it that way, but it is…"

"Then why is it killing me?' Gabriel asks with bitterness in his voice. Kristen releases him and sits back on the bed.

"I thought you had lung cancer."

"That's what they say because of the spots on my lungs," Gabriel says, in a soft tone again, "but I know what it is." Kristen gives him a confused look and urges him to continue. "Every time, just before they die, the air is knocked out of me and I have to breathe in deeply so not to choke. Every time, every single time, I feel something come into me. I think it's a part of their souls. And they're all killing me, eating away at me from the inside." Gabriel lowers his head down into his lap.

Kristen rubs the top of his head gently with her fingers. "I know what you're going through. It took me a long time to come to terms with the fact that my gift is going to kill me." She reaches down and touches his cheeks with her hands and lifts his head up. He looks at her, their faces inches from each other, with tears once again in his eyes.

"Are you not afraid of dying?"

Kristen smiles and gives a little laugh. "Of course I am. I'm scared shitless. But I also know that my life has had purpose and that I've helped a lot of people."

Staring into his eyes, Kristen suddenly leans forward and touches her lips to his. Gabriel doesn't kiss her back at first but then, very lightly, matches her intentions. The encounter is brief but when Kristen pulls herself away, there is a smile on Gabriel's face and the ocean blue has returned to his eyes. Kristen sees herself swimming in them.

"What was that for?" Gabriel asks, not breaking his smile.

"To show you that you're not alone," Kristen can't help but smile back at him, "I'm right here with you." Gabriel just stares at her, like this is something he's never experienced before. He reminds her of a child on Christmas morning. "I want to give you something. Give me your hand."

Gabriel looks down at his hand and when he looks back up, worry has replaced the smile that was there. "No," he says meekly in protest.

"I think I can make it work now that you're awake."

Gabriel continues to stare at her as she gestures for him to give her his hand. "I don't want to hurt you."

"Gabriel," she says, trying to muster up all of her reassurance, "I'm going to die, anyway. If this is my time then at least I die helping." She reaches for his hand but he pulls it away quickly.

"I will not be the cause of your death."

"Whatever happens, if I can heal you, then you are my legacy. Do you understand?" Gabriel shakes his head that he does not. "Everything you do from now on will be because of me. So, even if I'm not around to help people—which I won't be for much longer anyway—every person that you help will be because I allowed you to do so." Kristen smiles as she finishes. The uncertainty on Gabriel's face is apparent and grave. "This will be our greatest gift."

Gabriel looks at her and then down at his hands. He turns them over and stares at his palms and then clenches them both into tight fist.

Kristen reaches over and puts both her hands over one of his fists. "Are you ready?"

Gabriel shakes his head slowly. "No," he says weakly but relaxes his fist just enough for Kristen to open it and hold it with both hands.

Suddenly, heat surges through her entire body and she begins to shake. Her head begins to throb and she feels her heart beating faster than it ever has before. Then she feels the cold, creeping up her arms, going into chest and finally her head. Kristen is freezing as everything starts to fall away, by pieces at first and then darkness swallows them both. It feels empty and eternal but then there is a light that is blinding beyond comprehension and the warmth returns.

Gabriel opens his eyes and takes a deep breath. There is no pain. He smiles. But, looking down at his hand to see Kristen's loosely resting in his, Gabriel knows what has happened. He wants to mourn for her, he wants to cry and be angry at himself but he knows that she wouldn't want that. However, Gabriel does let a tear escape from his eyes as a light smile crosses his face. He bends over beside her ear and whispers, "Thank you," hoping that she can hear him, wherever she is.

"Well, hello, Gabriel," Dr. Jensen says as he walks into the room reading a chart. "So, what happened out there today..." the doctor stops speaking as he sees Kristen plopped over herself sitting cross-legged on the bed. "Is she okay?"

Gabriel can't control his tears then and they come flooding out. "No," he manages to get out in a low voice. "I don't think she is."

Dr. Jensen rushes over to the bedside and checks for a pulse in Kristen's neck. Gabriel already knew he wouldn't find one.

"Oh, God," he says and turns to the door. "Nurse!" he exclaims as he rushes out.

Gabriel gets off the bed, lightly putting his feet on the floor because he is unsure of his legs at the moment. Realizing he can stand, Gabriel bends over and kisses the top of Kristen's head softly. Hearing the sound of people running towards the room, Gabriel moves to the wall to give them all space as they come in. Occupied with Kristen, no one will notice him, at least for a minute. Gabriel leaves the room to go find Mr. Miller. To finish what he had started.

"Three things are necessary for the salvation of man: to know what he ought to believe; to know what he ought to desire; and to know what he ought to do."

~ Sir Thomas Aquinas

FAR FROM HEAVEN

A folded American flag is a piss-poor replacement for a brother. Feeling the red and white nylon and tracing its stars, Thomas Garret tosses the representation of another life lost on his brother's bed. Staring at the patriotic colors, Thomas wants to scream, wants to ask his brother if it was worth it.

Was it, Ben? Was it fucking worth it?

The outrage is all in his head, of course. The room is deathly still. Barely audible conversations make their way up the stairs from the kitchen and the living room—attempts to console the grieving and make sense of the situation. Suicide is a touchy subject.

Looking around the room, Thomas makes mental notes of everything the way it is—the way Ben had left things: A gray comforter over the bed neatly made, white sheets creased to perfection under the comforter. Three pairs of old sneakers and a new pair of combat boots barely stick out from under the bed. Ben's diploma framed on the wall next to a graduation photo of him and two friends whose names escape Thomas. Ben's dark oak desk stands in the corner by the window, almost baron save for a book or two from Ben's senior year. The dresser on the other side of the room, the same color as the desk, still contains Ben's clothes, which had been forgotten over the past three years but not discarded. Their mother didn't want anything changed in that room until Ben came safely back home, she wanted him to have something familiar.

It had been this way since he had joined the army but, until a few days ago, Thomas hadn't entered the room in over two years. He was still mad at Ben for leaving.

Thomas sits on the bed beside the flag and glares at it, trying to see past the fabric and find the essence of its meaning. Not actually having died in battle, Thomas doesn't know if his brother deserved a soldier's funeral. It is cold, but what if it was the truth? Thomas wonders if Ben had taken the easy way out; but, then again, it hadn't been that easy…

"Thomas?" His thoughts are interrupted by his mother's voice from the doorway. Looking up from the flag, he sees the sadness that her eyes have been trying to hide for the past four days. "Are you okay?"

"Yeah, I'm okay," Thomas begins with lies for his mother's sake, "How are you?"

She moves slowly to the bed and sits down beside him, seeing that the flag is on the bed as well. "I've been better," she delivers the words through a sigh.

Thomas reaches his arm slowly across his mother and lets his hand fall on her shoulder lightly, something resembling a hug. She simply gives his hand a pat and then seemingly forgets that it's there. They sit together like this in agreeable silence for what seems like an eternity, neither saying anything nor knowing what to say. Thomas opens his mouth and waits for something to come out, anything, when he is interrupted by footsteps ascending the stairs.

"Connie?" Thomas' father calls out into the open air.

"In here, Don," his mother says barely loud enough to be heard outside the room.

His father reaches the last step and looks to his right into Thomas' room and then, not seeing anyone, turns his head to look into the open doorway of Ben's room and sees the two of them on the bed.

"Oh," he blinks and slides back down the stairs by a step, "Connie, your mother is looking for you."

Thomas' mother sniffs and rubs her eyes. "Tell her I'll be down in just a sec."

"Okay." He turns to walk back downstairs but then turns back, as if he forgot something. He stares through the open door and Thomas feels his father's eyes on him. "How you doing, champ?" The question is quiet and filled with practiced concern.

"I'm okay, dad."

His father gives a small, quick smile and then walks down the stairs. His mother gives the same smile and also a quick hug before she gets off the bed. At the door, she turns and stands in the frame. "Don't stay up here too long, okay, honey?"

"Sure, mom," Thomas says with reassurance and then watches as she walks down the stairs.

Thomas lies back on the bed, letting his legs hang off the side, and stares up at the dismal, bland ceiling with its decorative cracks and small water damage spots. "You fucker," he whispers into the air as he runs his fingers across the flag.

That night around the dinner table, after all of the traces of the sympathetic mourners were gone, the somberness of the day stays with Thomas and his parents. As Thomas prods at some left over casserole with his fork, his parents sit and stare into the ethereal nothingness that resides between them all. He understands that they're tired and now, with no one left to put the brave face on for, they can let it show. None of them have even changed out of their funeral clothes.

"Thomas," his mother breaks the silence in a meek voice, "you need to eat something."

Thomas looks up and into his mother's eyes and sees that something is missing and realizes her eyes will never look the same. "You're not eating."

She looks down at her own untouched plate, blinks and then a second later the tears start to tumble out as she cries, like she always does, without making a sound. Thomas watches his mother get up from the table and head toward the living room.

"Shit, mom, I'm sorry." She holds up a hand and tries to say something but can't. Thomas looks to his father who has been eyeballing his meatloaf since it's been on his plate and has finally put a small piece onto his fork and is about to take the bite but decides against it and puts his fork down.

"I need a cigarette," his father says and stands up, fondling the pack out of his pocket and going for the kitchen door.

Once again, like on so many nights, Thomas is left alone at the table. The only difference is that on most other nights there is some kind of soft music filling the room but tonight no one could think of anything appropriate to play.

Thomas sits back against his chair and looks around at the empty chairs and thinks about how, now that everything is changed, in regards to this kitchen it seems like nothing has changed. Looking at the chair to his left—Ben's chair—Thomas thinks back to the week before and the first night Ben had been back home on leave. Thomas had seen it then, something wrong in Ben's eyes. He knew that something terrible had happened, or was going to happen.

+++

Thomas was secretly excited for days when he had heard that Ben was coming home and that excitement had become particularly hard to contain when they were on the way to the airport to pick Ben up. Waiting outside the arrival gate, Thomas tried to keep his cool but his feet wouldn't stop fidgeting. And then there he was, walking toward them in head-to-toe green digital camouflage, wearing the same haircut and the same uniform as the day he left and yet, something was missing. As Ben got closer Thomas realized that he wasn't smiling that perfectly white, cocky smile that he always wore. All that Thomas saw on Ben's face as he stepped in front of them and hugged their parents was a strange kind of sadness.

That night at dinner things hadn't gotten any better. Ben had barely uttered a word to any of them. In the car the radio distracted them from the silence and when they got home, Ben went directly to his room and stayed there until called to eat. They all sat in their usual places: Their father and Ben at the two ends of the rectangular table, Thomas and his mother directly across from one another on the sides. The perfect distance where no one was close enough to touch anyone else. Their parents had the usual conversations and quibbled over the mundane. Thomas sat and watched as Ben devoured his food with military precision. After Ben was done he stayed around for a few minutes to finish his Bud Light and then he quietly excused himself and went back upstairs, leaving Thomas alone with his thoughts as his parents continued talking.

The days that followed were the same. It was a week into his leave and Ben had still barely spoken to Thomas, which was strange. They hadn't always gotten along but they had always been able to talk to one another, laugh and pal around. Ben had helped Thomas through his first bad break up. Not being able to talk to his brother was something that Thomas had never experienced and he didn't know how to deal with it.

"What's wrong with you?" Thomas asked Ben one day as he watched his brother cleaning a pistol on his bed.

"Nothing is wrong with me," Ben said as he examined the inner workings of his killing machine like a surgeon examines the insides of a patient, "what's wrong with you?" He asked Thomas, without looking up.

"Nothing," Thomas replied quickly, a bit taken aback by the question, "I'm fine."

Ben looked up at his brother then, running his eyes over Thomas to see if he was lying, but then looked back down without saying a word. The gun required more attention. Thomas walked out of the room without a sound.

That night Thomas was in the middle of a fitful sleep over run with dreams of falling through the air with a parachute that wouldn't open and then being trapped in a car that was submerged in water. He snapped awake as he felt the water enter his lungs and sat up in his bed with a gasp.

It was pitch black in his room, no light from the moon coming through his window. Thomas steadied himself with a few deep breaths and then felt his spine perk up with the realization that he wasn't alone. Not waiting to see if the presence was just remnants of a fearful dream, Thomas reached over and turned on the lamp that was on his nightstand. With the new light added to the room, the shadows crawled back into their hiding places and all that was left was Ben, sitting in the arm chair adjacent to the bed, watching Thomas with unblinking eyes and holding his pistol.

"How long have you been here?" Thomas asked after the shock settled into his stomach.

"Awhile," Ben said calmly, without moving a muscle.

"Why?"

"I heard sounds, thought I'd check to see that you were okay." He said and let his pistol rest on the arm of the chair.

"No, I'm fine," Thomas said as he rubbed his eyes, "I just had some bad dreams."

"Yeah, me too," Ben said, finally moving his eyes away from Thomas as he looked around the room, as if he hadn't seen it in years. "They're about the only kind I have."

Thomas let his words hang in the air, unaware of what to say to his brother. "Do you want to talk about them?"

Ben's eyes snapped back to Thomas and he didn't know what he saw in them, but Thomas was afraid. "No," he said and stood up, gripping his pistol as to not leave it behind. "Go back to sleep."

And then he was gone. His room was just across the hall but, to Thomas, the distance felt unreachable. Thomas turned the lamp off and settled himself back into his covers, preparing himself for the rest of the sleepless night.

The next morning at breakfast everything was as usual: Father reading the newspaper, mother rambling on to someone over the phone and the brothers eating their food in relative silence. Nothing was mentioned about the previous night or the clear changes in Ben's personality. If their parents noticed, they said nothing and had no plans on finding out or trying to help him. Thomas ate his eggs and remembered the mornings, long past gone, when voices filled the room and there was always a smile on his brother's face.

Dinner that night felt like a replica of all the other dinners they had shared since Ben had gotten back. There was food mixed in with silence and all of it wrapped in a feeling of unavoidable dread. After inquiring about Thomas' day at school, their mother was occupied with other thoughts and their father ate his food oblivious to other things that were or were not happening.

"Hey," Ben said quietly to Thomas, as if coming out of a fog, "sorry about last night, man. I didn't mean to freak you out."

Thomas stared into his brother's eyes, seeing something of his former self in them. "It's okay," Thomas quietly replied. "It's nice to know you got my back," he cracked a smile, "in case I was in trouble."

Ben just smiled and reached over, ruffling Thomas' hair quickly and then returned his attention to his plate. Thomas did the same, staring at his pasta and thinking that things were going to be okay.

+++

The funeral processions had been exhausting and Thomas couldn't fight back the gloom and tiredness any longer. Walking up the stairs and loosening his tie, Thomas yawns and feels like he might collapse before he makes it all the way up. Stopping on the top step, he stares into his brother's room. For the entirety of the time that Ben was overseas they had kept the door to his room shut but now, here it stood open for all to see into. Almost as if his parents wanted the room to be accessible if Ben's soul wanted to return to it. If Ben's soul was looking for somewhere to go, Thomas didn't think that it would come back to this house.

Lying on the bed in his room, Thomas gazes at the ceiling in the dim light of his lamp, waiting to see the blood splatter that had appeared on Ben's ceiling just a few days ago. After the investigating officers came and went and the coroner took away Ben's body, the splatter on the ceiling and some arterial spray on the back wall were all that was left of him. After a night of hearing his mother cry, trying to console her and watching his father chain smoke, the next day finally came and with it came the cleaning.

+++

Thomas stood on one of the dining room chairs and scrubbed furiously at the dark stain on the ceiling with a brillo pad that had some sort of ammonia based product on it. The smell of the cleaner or the sight of the blood not wanting to come off of the ceiling was making Thomas a bit dizzy; he couldn't decide which. Maybe it was both.

Thomas stood on the chair and scrubbed until his arm felt numb and he didn't think his fingers would ever uncoil. Just as he was about to give up and hurl himself from the chair onto the bed, a flake from the part of the ceiling that he had been cleaning loosened itself from the rest of the mess and Thomas watched as a breeze from the open window broke it free. The flake swayed from side to side as it fell, doing a slow motion dance with the air. Thomas followed it with his eyes as it was trying to find the ground and, for a reason unknown to him, Thomas held out his hand and the flake settled into his palm—quietly and with a serene sense of calm. Looking down at the dark red and brown piece of ceiling he realized that this insignificant thing was all that was left of his brother, the blood he left behind to remind Thomas of what had happened. When a teardrop fell into his palm was the moment Thomas realized he was crying. He hadn't cried yet—he didn't think he'd be able to.

+++

Thomas snaps awake from a dream where he was stranded in a desert, the sun beating down on him, killing him slowly. But instead of sand, the desert was filled with gunpowder and loneliness. Surrounded by darkness, he takes in slow, deep breaths to steady his vision. His feet know what he is going to do before his mind does. It is dark and as he walks towards the door, guided by fading moonlight, a severe case of déjà vu washes over him and he shutters at the thought. His bedroom door opens with the same slight creak that is deafening in the silence and it's the same number of steps to Ben's door. The only difference is that tonight the door is already open and Ben is not sitting on his bed, mumbling to himself with his pistol in his hands.

+++

"Do you wanna know how it feels?" Ben asked through the darkness as Thomas stood in the open doorway.

Thomas made small steps towards the bed. "How what feels?"

Ben held up the pistol for Thomas to inspect in the forlorn light coming from the moon. "Having the power of God." The pistol gleamed as Thomas fixed his gaze on it.

"I don't think God's in there, Ben," Thomas said and sat down next to his brother.

"You don't?" Ben brought the pistol down and rested it on his knee, never taking his eyes off of the metal. "This is a Beretta M9 9mm and my guardian angel. Its protection gives me life, its bullets give others death—it decides who lives and dies."

"You mean you decide." Thomas said, trying to understand.

Ben finally shifted his gaze to his brother. "By extension," he said with something that seemed sinister in his eyes. "Do you want to hold it?"

Thomas looked at Ben who motioned his head toward the gun and then slowly moved his hand until the instrument of death was resting in front of Thomas. With an unsteady hand Thomas gripped the handle and felt its full weight ripple throughout his body. He stared at the pistol in his hand, examining every line and sleek curve and he wondered how easy the trigger was to pull.

"How does it feel?" Ben asked, not looking at Thomas.

"Good," Thomas said, not taking his eyes off of the metal. "It feels good."

"I'm glad," Ben took in a deep breath and let it out slowly. "It's gotten too heavy for me," he finished almost with a laugh.

Thomas looked up at Ben who was staring back at him. The sinister aspects of his eyes had disappeared when the pistol left his hand. "How many people has it killed?" Thomas could hear the wonderment in his own voice. Ben looked away then.

"How many?" He looked up at the ceiling, apparently counting the death toll in his head. "That gun...eleven," he said in a matter-of-fact tone, as if he were counting anything else besides people who were no longer alive.

Thomas looked to the gun and then back to his brother. "How many people have *you* killed?"

Ben's head dropped and his shoulders seemed to sag under the weight of the question and his eyes fixated on the fibers of the carpet. "I lost count a long time ago."

Thomas stared at Ben then, really looked at him—through the strong will and glossy finish of the soldier—and saw his brother for the first time in what seemed like forever as tears rolled down his cheeks.

"There's nothing there," Ben said through quiet sobs.

"There's nothing where?"

"There's nothing there," the sobs were getting louder, "out in the middle of nowhere, oil fires tearing through the dark sky, lighting up the sand and darkness just enough so you can keep walking." Ben wiped his eyes and gave a slight chuckle. "Sometimes I thought we'd walk into oblivion, but at least that'd be an end. A way to stop it all." The tears continued to fall.

"We don't have to talk about this if you don't want to," Thomas whispered, sensing his own hesitation to Ben's new openness.

Ben turned his head slowly and looked at Thomas without really looking *at* him. "It's all a lie, everything they tell you—your liberties, the choices you can make, your purpose," he cracked a small smile, "what you're fighting for, prepared to die for. It's all bullshit." His eyes seemed to focus then. "You can see that can't you?"

"What happened to you over there?" Thomas asked, hearing his own brazen disgust.

Ben's smiled faded and Thomas saw the light dim in his pale eyes. "You asked me about my dreams the other night." He let his words trail off into the still air.

"Yeah?"

Ben looked away, putting his face into his hands and then furiously rubbed his eyes. "I see their faces," he said almost without sound, "every time I close my eyes, I see their faces."

"Whose faces?" Thomas moved a little closer to Ben.

"It's not what you think," Ben continued as the sobs returned, louder than before. "It's not what I thought. I don't know what I expected, what I imagined when…some distant battlefield with unidentifiable enemies." He drew in a breath. "They were close, they were all so close." The tears fell hard and Thomas thought he heard the beginnings of a wail in Ben's throat. "Their eyes, the way everything seems to fade away and it's never coming back and, you know that you've caused this." A long pause filled with soft sobs muffled by Ben's hands splintered the suffocating silence in the room. "That's what I see when I sleep." He finally said.

"Ben, I'm so sorry," but Thomas was unable to find the words, unable to understand enough to console so he just put his arm just his brother and let him cry.

Ben looked towards the window. "There were sermons, there were sermons every Sunday. In this little fucking shanty building on the outskirts of the base." Ben let out a tiny chuckle in remembrance. "The Chaplin was this quirky little guy, always smiling and telling jokes. Everybody liked him."

"I didn't think you believed in all that."

Ben let out another light chuckle. "I never did before and I gotta tell ya, at first it didn't make any sense out there. But after a while," he took in a breath and exhaled slowly, "it became a way to hide away from everything. A small solace in a sea of never ending shit." Ben wiped the tears from his eyes. "There was so much talk of Heaven and Hell, how to get into one and avoid the other. To make it make sense we try to give them physical locations—Heaven above us and Hell below us. As if we could actually travel there. It makes it more real, more obtainable, more frightening. Do you understand?"

Ben finally looked at his brother then but all Thomas could do was nod in an odd reverence.

"Rationally speaking, Hell is the farthest you can be from Heaven. The farthest you can be from peace and understanding. But that's wrong; we can't be any farther from Heaven than we are right now. When push comes to shove, when our true selves are revealed, we're nothing but wolves devouring one another. And it will always be like this until we are all, every last one of us, dust in the desert."

"Ben..."

"You have to help me."

"Anything," Thomas said, eager to be his brother's savior.

Ben reached over slowly and took hold of Thomas' hand which is still holding the pistol. Thomas looked to Ben, into his brother's eyes, only to see the sadness which had resided in them for so long now.

"Help me find peace," he pleaded in a soft voice.

Thomas looked to the pistol and then back to Ben's face— the moon light coming through the window illuminating his pain.

"No," Thomas whispered at first, and then louder and with more conviction, "No, I can't let you do that."

"I can't do it, I've tried and I can't. That's why I need you."

The way Ben said 'need' sent shivers through Thomas' spine. Ben had never needed anything. He had always been the strong one, the one to turn to. He could always do what was needed of *him*. Thomas had always assumed that's why he had joined the service.

Ben sat through the seconds of silence and, when not hearing protest, he untangled Thomas' hand from the pistol, replaced it with his own, and raised the barrel to his forehead and put Thomas' finger on the trigger. Thomas watched his brother in stunned horror.

"I can't do this," Thomas felt tears of his own coming now, mimicking his brother's in every way. "I need you here with me."

"I'll always be with you. Nothing can take me away from you." The words came out of Ben and floated into the air above everything else that was happening. "Not even death."

Thomas was shaking more than he thought was possible as his vision began to blur from the tears being shed and falling with reckless abandon. "I can't," Thomas whispered while his finger rested on the trigger. "You can't ask me to."

"You're the only one I can ask," Ben's whisper matched Thomas'. "You're all I got." He whimpered and gripped Thomas' hand tighter against the pistol. "I need you to be strong, stronger than I could ever be."

Ben then lowered the pistol slightly and, with his other hand, grabbed Thomas tight and pulled him into a warm embrace. Thomas let his tears soak Ben's shoulder as he held his brother with a ferocity he didn't know he possessed. "I love you," was all that he could say.

"Thank you," Ben said as he pulled away. "I love you too, brother."

And with that, Ben grabbed the pistol and thrust it hard under his chin, pointing the barrel towards the ceiling. Thomas put his finger on the trigger and squeezed softly with the weight of the impact. The sound thundered through the room and split his ear drums as Thomas watched what happened in slow motion: The barrel sliding back, the flash coming quickly from the muzzle and Ben's head snapping back with an unknown amount of force as the bullet ripped through his head and then exited through his skull; red liquid, bone fragments and brain matter following the same course.

It seemed to Thomas to take forever to wash the blood off of his face and neck and out of his hair. When his parents had found Thomas he was curled up in a ball in front of Ben's bed, shaking violently and drenched in red. Questions had been asked but Thomas had been unable to answer. Because the gun was resting beside Ben's lifeless hand, and the way the bullet had went through his head, the police had concluded suicide. Later, when Thomas had regained his voice, a tired looking officer had asked him for a statement.

"It happened so fast," was all that Thomas had been able to tell the man. "It happened so fast."

+++

Thomas lies on Ben's bed, trying to feel his essence but everything is gone from the room. All that's left is what's in his head, the memories that he possesses. But now even those are tainted. Every time Thomas thinks about Ben, whether it be about them playing together in the back yard or watching one of his baseball games, the thoughts all eventually come back to the same thing: Thomas watching the life fade from Ben's eyes as the ringing continues in his ears and the red runs down the wall.

Thomas sits up and stares into the nothingness of the late hour, trying to summon something from within himself, hoping that he has the strength his brother didn't. Ben's parting gift had been his own curse—by setting Ben free, Thomas had trapped himself. Every time Thomas closes his eyes he sees Ben's face, but not always at his moment of death. Sometimes Thomas sees Ben laugh or smile or he's just looking back at Thomas with a calmness on his face that gives hope. Thomas closes his eyes once more. *Ben, don't worry, I am strong.* And he smiles.

TEMPLE HILL RD.

It's the place where everyone goes. It just sits there on its plateau, overlooking the town, looming over the people. There always seems to be something going on up there. Every night, after 7 P.M., you will barely find a person or a vehicle on our cracking pavement and pot-hole infested streets. But those lights from the temple are burning bright, like a beacon. But I suppose that's the desired effect.

We have no crime in our lovely, little, boring, mind-fucking town. No garbage litters Main Street and there is no graffiti on the buildings. Well, not for a long time anyway. Not since I was a little boy. The McDermott family moved here ten years ago when I was seven. They came from some big city on the East Coast. I forget which one. Mr. McDermott, Edward, used to be a televangelist. His wife, Susan, was a stay at home mother. Then there were the two children—Matthew, who was two years older than me, and Lily, who was my age. They were the perfect All-American family and modern day missionaries. They came to our town in hopes of transforming the heathens of lower class middle America into outstanding, Protestant citizens and they had most of the town in their vice grip for close to a decade, using us as marionettes—pulling the strings and watching us dance for their own entertainment. That was, until last night, when the temple burned to the ground.

α

"What do you think they do up there?" Sarah, my best friend since we were three, once asked me. I took a hit of the joint we were sharing, inhaled slowly and then exhaled forcibly, a series of coughs followed. Sitting on a dilapidated stone wall overlooking the highway, this was how we spent our afternoons.

"Brain-washing," I told her once I recovered. "Mind control." I took another small drag from the joint. "And ritualistic killings."

Choosing to rebel against the temple at the age of fourteen, this was what our lives had become: Seventeen years old and outcasts from everything we've known. I handed the joint back to her and she looked at me with dismay through her mossy-green eyes.

"Ritualistic killings? Really?" She asked as she took the joint from my hand. The moments where our fingers briefly and lightly touched sent electricity throughout my entire body. The only times I ever truly felt alive.

"Yep," I said and watched her light pink lips suck in smoke. "What do you think happened to Mr. Snyder?" She paused on her second inhalation and looked at me again, her dark hair circling her face with the wind, engulfing it at times so all that you can see are those eyes.

"I thought he drove drunk into a tree?" She removed the hair from her face, took another hit and then handed me the dwindling joint.

"Sure, he did," I took a long drag and exhaled slowly this time. "After having his organs and genitals removed."

Sarah smiled—the kind of smile that I hoped she only showed me—gave a little laugh and a playful shove to my shoulder. I handed her back the now almost non-existent joint. Through her smile she inhaled the last bit of pot and the flicked the rest of the paper into the shrubs. After a moment of staring at the vague passing cars on the highway the smile faded from her face.

"Do you think they really do that?"

I followed her gaze to the temple beaming on its pedestal. With its domed, cathedral ceilings, towering crucifix steeple and large windows it looked like a monster waiting to eat anything that came near it.

"Yea," I said as I stood up on the wall and offered Sarah my hand. "Maybe."

With her fingers draped over mine and squeezing ever so lightly, I pulled her to her feet and she let go of my hand and walked ahead of me. I felt dead again.

α

As we watched the temple burn, Sarah and I stood hand and hand. The way the flames and smoke mixed with the dark night skyline to create a serene shade of purple that I had never seen before, it was the most romantic thing I had ever witnessed. Sarah, grasping my hand so hard I thought I would die if she let go, turned and looked at me. Her eyes were dimly lit from the distant fire and I could see the pupils swimming in her irises. With her hair blowing in front of her face she leaned into me and kissed my lips with the lightest touch and only for a second, but just for that second, I was home.

"I love you." She said and then turned back to watch the crumbling idol upon the plateau.

Still looking at her I whispered, "I always have." She squeezed my hand again and I felt the breath leave my body.

α

Things began to change when the McDermott's came to town. My family started attending church services, for one. Our town had never had too much need for church—there was a small Zionist movement that congregated in an old warehouse on the outskirts of town. Sometimes strange music could be heard coming from there. Out of just over the four thousand people that inhabited the town, the Church of Zion had only about thirty or so members, not enough to make a fuss about.

I remember learning about the first pilgrims and their coming to the New World for so-called religious freedom. Seemed to me like just a bunch of rebellious heathens trying to break their way out of the system and become "unaccounted for." And that's basically the mentality I had about my environment and the people that were shaping it.

My father was the town sheriff and a part of the city council. So naturally, not long after the McDermott's moved into their modest, two-story, white picket fenced house on Birch Court, our door was the one of the first they came knocking on to spread the word of their ministry.

"I don't have much time for your nonsense." Was what my father said, at first, as he exhaled the smoke from his cigarette into Edward McDermott's face. Edward, standing there on our porch in his navy blue J. Crew sweater and khaki slacks, he just smiled his perfect, shit-eating smile through the smoke at my father. Susan, in her teal sundress, had her arms around the children at her sides—parading them to us as trophies, like they had won a "Best Family" contest.

I didn't pay much attention to Lily, at first. All I saw was Matthew, with his blue sweater and khakis that were almost identical to his father's. All I wanted to do was to lunge at him, knock him into the yard and mess up that perfectly combed, blonde hair of his with the noogie of a life time. But, of course, I curbed this desire and just looked down at my dirty, bare feet.

When Edward asked why my father didn't worship the lord, he simply replied that in his line of work, even in this town, he had seen more than enough to know that God didn't give a shit. Those were his exact words; I'll never be able to forget them.

However, Mr. McDermott being the persistent man that he was, continued knocking on our door in attempts to brainwash my father so that he could use his sway in the community to convince people to listen to what the new preacher in town had to say. About a month after coming to town, Mr. McDermott bought an old factory and the land with it and turned it into The Church of the Protestant God. It drew in a small congregation at first, mostly people who were just curious. Six months after he opened the church doors, over half of the town was eating out of the palms of his hands, like trained fucking dogs.

As a prominent member of the town, my father eventually had to stop ignoring the man. Still skeptical, at first, he took everything he heard in with defensive ears. I remember how he used to talk about Mr. McDermott at the dinner table—how he didn't like his boisterous, propaganda bullshit and what it was doing to this town. But I can still remember the day that changed his mind.

"Sit down, son." He told me while pulling out one of the dining room chairs for me and then taking up one beside me. Holding my hand, which is something he never did, my father looked into my face and I saw a tear lingering in his dark brown eye. This also, he never did.

"It's your mother," he stopped there and drew in a lung full of air. "Your mother," stopping again, but this time he had to turn away to hide the actual tear he thought I didn't see tumbling down his cheek. Taking in another breath, he tried again. "Your mother has cancer."

As if a gunshot went off right beside my head, my ears began to ring. As my father's lips moved I clinched my body in anticipation for the ringing to subside, but its force only grew. By the time my father was bear hugging me with lung crushing power, I thought my ears might burst and I began to cry. I cried as much for my mother's decaying life as for the thought of my father having to watch blood run from my ears.

I was eight years old and expected to take the news of my mother's condition with stride, to watch her die slowly with ambivalent strength and silence. My father took to prayer at The Church of the Protestant God, under the wing of *Edward*. He started spending the majority of his time at the church, when he wasn't working. My mother went with him because she said that it helped my father cope. She was the only one with any real strength in the face of her death.

A little over a year after my mother's diagnosis, she went in to a remission. It was a goddamn miracle, or so everyone said. Her recovery was the catalyst for the temple—it convinced my father and the whole rest of the fucking town of the power of God. Everyone wanted to go to the church where your prayers are answered. The old warehouse would no longer adequately serve the people. Expansions had to be made. The plans for The Temple of the Reformed were underway.

Mr. McDermott bought the land that used to be a drive-in theatre, but over the years had been reduced to a grassy parking lot and a dilapidated screen. Some of the town's kids still drove up there to do what kids do. Its nickname was "hump hill" but the actual name of the street was Harvey Circle. That changed just like everything else. It became Temple Hill Rd, and nothing would ever be the same.

α

The day before the temple burned down was the one year anniversary of the day that Sarah's mother killed herself. Three years ago, when we were fourteen, Sarah's father had lost his job. Ending up—as most of the town's people had—a God-fearing Christian, he was confused as to the reason for his bad luck. In a warped sense of delusion, he began to blame Sarah's mother: she didn't go to the temple to worship and pray like she should, like God deserved and demanded, so he was being punished. They began to fight all of the time, over anything and everything. She refused to go to the temple just because he had lost his job and he refused to look for another until she became the woman she should be. This became an everyday event in Sarah's world and they never stopped their arguing on mine or Sarah's account. Sarah never said anything but I knew that her heart and spirit were breaking. To get her away from her parents, I started taking her to the stone wall to spend our afternoons.

It was my fault Sarah wasn't at home the day her mother killed herself. Sarah wasn't feeling well and wanted to go home after school was over but I told her that she would be better off hanging out with me, that she didn't want to go to her house just to listen to the yelling. It had been over two years since her father had lost his job and her mother had spent the last few months in a catacomb depression due to his constant hammering on her character and worth as a human being and as a mother. Everything has its breaking point, I guess after two years on constant fighting and self-loathing, their fight that morning had been her mother's. Sarah once told me that she blamed herself for not being there to comfort her mother, to reassure her of her importance in Sarah's life. I told her we can't blame ourselves for other people's mistakes. She just broke down and cried.

We celebrated the anniversary by skipping school to stay at her house and look through photos of Sarah and her mother. Conrad, Sarah's father, would never know because he spent his days at the temple. Picture after picture, her mother staring at us with Sarah's eyes; smiling that smile that only Sarah's presence could create. My chest ached over my own breaking heart—I wanted to cry as much for Sarah losing her mother as for me still having my own. I wanted to comfort Sarah, to tell her that she was strong and that we could get through this together but the pictures were all that she wanted. And while she poured through album after album, I couldn't help but continually turning my gaze to the living room rug—a light shade of gray that matched the walls. It'd been washed and scrubbed a dozen times, but I can still imagine the dark red pool that seeped deep into the carpet's fibers. We found her, me and Sarah. We found her lying on the rug, still holding the shinny metal revolver, a small blood dripping hole going into her left temple and a large, oozing canyon coming out of her right. Her eyes were staring straight, straight up at God, unflinching in defiance. I guess we all have our own path to peace.

"Looking at pictures of the dead," Sarah told me as she lightly traced the outline of her mother in a photograph, "is like trying to find a soul lost in the aftermath of life."

She continued to look at her mother through the slick feel of the photo. I stared at her face, studying her every expression—looking for the exact moment that she felt happiness, love, and sadness. I watched her eyes as she searched for meaning in her mother's smile.

"It's almost impossible to find," Sarah said as she placed the photo back into its rightful place in the album, "but we have to try, don't we?" She turned to me with her tear glistened eyes and any reserve that I had was torn down in that instant.

"Yes," I said as my eyes unlocked the flood gates. "Yes." We spent the afternoon crying into one another's shoulders.

α

When I was eleven, the doors to The Temple of the Reformed opened. My family, like most of the families in town, frequented the place of worship perched above on its plateau. I attended with a subdued perspective on religion. I didn't want to be there but my parents wanted me to be and I hadn't yet discovered the serenity of rebellion.

At the age of twelve, however, newly developed hormones kicked into high gear and the natural scent of Lily McDermott seemed to be pheromones that had been engineered specifically for me. Even at that age, I knew the difference between love and infatuation—my heart was already reserved for Sarah. But she didn't see me, at least, not the way that I saw her.

Lily didn't see me either. My father pulled a lot of respect in our little town but we were still on the poor side of the tracks. Lily, in her posh Sunday dresses and catalogue play clothes, always seemed to look straight through my tattered second-hand store jeans and dirty tank tops. There's nothing worse than being invisible in plain sight. I felt somehow less than human. Even at that age, I wondered if I was actually real, or just someone's sad dream.

Sunday after Sunday I quietly pined, or so I thought, for Lily. After two years, it was quite common knowledge where my affections lie. The adults thought it was cute. The other kids made fun of me and Sarah despised me for it. I think she knew the truth before I did. Lily still didn't look at me.

And then one Sunday something changed. I don't know if it was something new in the air or the fact that I wore the new church suit my Grandmother had sent me or if Lily had just decided to open her eyes, but something changed.

"Hi." A quiet but resonating voice came from behind me. It sounded as if the sky had opened up and a seraph was speaking directly to me. I turned to gaze into Lily's unnerving blue eyes. She wore a dark green band in her perfectly straightened, strawberry blonde hair to match her dress. I thought her, indeed, an angel. She belonged at the right hand of a celestial throne singing worship songs, not talking to me in a downstairs hallway of a temple, waiting in line to use the bathroom.

"Hey, Lily," I was surprised that words actually made it from behind my lips. I don't know if she was shy or if my gaze was too steady but she looked down slightly and to my side.

"How come you've never said 'hello' to me?" She asked in a sheepish, low-pitch, pitiful voice that would make anyone malleable in her hands. I was dumbfounded by the question.

"I didn't think I was anyone you would want saying 'hello' to you," was all that I could think to say.

Regaining her confidence, she looked up at me again, her eyes gleaming in the dim hallway light.

"Of course I would," a slick smile crossed her face. She had perfect, white teeth. "I've been waiting for me to speak to me for a long time."

Once again, dumbfounded, all I could do was grin my big, stupid grin back at her—thankful that I had brushed my teeth that morning. We heard light footsteps on the staircase nearest to us. She brought herself close to me and, standing on her toes, leaned into my ear.

"Ride your bike to my house this afternoon after my father's done preaching."

The warmth of her breath on my ear seemed to draw all of the blood in my body to my head. And when she backed away, it retreated with her to a somewhat lower region.

"Ok?" She asked still holding the smile on her face. All I could do was continue to grin and nod my head quickly in response. She subdued her smile a bit and then walked by me to go to the stairs, gently brushing my arm with her fingers as she went, perking up all of the hairs. I watched her disappear up the stairs and let out a giant breath, as if I hadn't been breathing for the entire encounter. Maybe I hadn't.

I didn't own a bike, but Sarah did. A shiny black, eighteen speed mountain bike with red racing stripes on the body. Asking to use it was a bit more than awkward. Sarah hated Lily McDermott, and she hated the part of me that wanted her. I pleaded and pleaded and she finally relented, like a parent who knew that I was going to do what I wanted one way or another.

The house on Birch Court looked the same this time as it had the previous hundreds of time I had passed it. The white picket fence barricaded the perfectly trimmed front yard. Beyond the yard lay the house, a light shade of yellow unlike any others on the street, a matching two car garage stood a few feet on the side. All of the windows adorned red shutters and drapes. I sat in the street on Sarah's bike, inches away from the yard, unaware of what to do next. I felt as if the fence had a lock on it and I didn't have the combination to get in. Luckily, to my relief, Lily poked her head out the front door and promptly waved me over. Reminding myself to breathe, I hoped off the bike, opened the fence gate and slowly made my way to what seemed to be another world.

"Put your bike behind the garage," she said, still with only her head poking out from behind the big, wooden door.

Stowing my bike out of sight, I trotted back to the front door which was left only slightly ajar. I slipped inside, closing the door behind me, and was greeted by cavernous white walls. A crystal chandelier hung ten feet above my head in what I perceived to be the living room. I scanned the room to the right and found Lily waiting on a winding staircase, leaning against the railing. Staring at her, I was still unaware of what to do next.

"Come on up, silly" she said with a smile and then proceeded to bound up the stairs.

"Where's your dad?" I asked as I ascended the stairs in a daze of wonderment. The carpet was an off-white color that seemed inviting but also unsettling at the same time. With the white walls, I imagined it was what an asylum must look like.

"My father and mother are in meetings at the temple." She said from somewhere out of sight.

"And Matthew?" She came into view just as I found the last step, standing beside a door a few feet from me.

"He's taking a nap," she indicated a door down the hall with a nod and opened the door she was standing beside. "You wanna see my room?" And she bounded inside.

Like a zombie, I walked into her room, not knowing what to expect but hungry for something none the less. She was sitting on her bed and patting the spot beside her, indicating me to sit. I felt like a dog following instructions but I was okay with it.

Her room was the same white as all of the other walls in the house. No posters hung on her walls. It was as if her world was devoid of color. Even her bed sheets were white.

"So, what do you think?" She sounded as if my nervousness had somehow affected her.

"I like it." Lies always seem good at a moment of truth.

"My father says that I shouldn't consort with you," she said as she inched herself closer to me, "because you haven't yet seen the light. That you don't feel God's love." Leaning closer so she was only inches from my face, she clasped her hand over mine and kissed my cheek lightly. "You feel God's love, don't you?"

With her kisses moving down to my neck, I felt the eternal flames of an inferno towering inside of my soul; engulfing my entirety, leaving only my heart still beating. All other sounds—the birds conversing outside of the window, dogs barking in the distance, the car parking in the driveway, the downstairs door opening, the footsteps on the stairs—were lost in the void of everything else that didn't matter. All that did matter were her lips as they were moving ever so close to mine.

A knock at the door. A panic that I had never felt before turned my blood cold and made my heart beat even faster. Lily calmly turned her head to the door, seeming to have been half expecting the terrifying intrusion.

"Lily?" The voice of the Reverend McDermott floated through the door. I wanted to vomit.

"Just a second, Daddy." She got up from the bed and moved quickly to open her closet door and motioned me inside with a stern finger. All of this she did with an expressionless face.

With me safely hidden inside her closet, Lily went to open the door. I watched through tilted slits in her closet doors.

"Hey, Daddy," she said in a light-hearted-good-girl voice she had obviously perfected. "How was the meeting?"

Reverend McDermott stepped through the threshold and scanned the room as if he expected to see something else other than Lily.

"It was fine, dear," he said as he satisfied his search and then lightly patted her on the head. "We ended early to attend to some other business." He walked to the doorway and stopped in the middle of it, gazing out of the room towards the stairs.

"You have a special visitor." He motioned with his index finger for whoever was out there to come into the room.

After a moment, a man stepped into the room. He was wearing a crisp, brown suit with shiny brown shoes. From my position in the closet, I could see that his hair was thinning on top and turning slightly gray. He had a full mustache resting atop his lips and the stubble of a day or two away from a razor. It was his eyes that I recognized—those dark and desolate orbs that seemed so vacant it hurt to look into them. Mr. Douglas, he had set hidden in the middle pews at the temple for as long as I had been in attendance. Never saying a word, only mumbling in prayer at the appropriate times. He stood there staring at Lily with those eyes. Something danced in them, a glimmer of something that hadn't been there in a very long time. A ghost haunting his eyes with desire. I've never hated anyone more than I did at that moment.

"Well, I've got some work to attend to downstairs," Reverend McDermott said and bent down to kiss Lily gently on the head.

Turning, Reverend McDermott paused to look at Mr. Douglas who immediately produced a sweaty wad of bills from his pocket. Reverend McDermott took the money, skimmed over the amount and gave the smile I had seen him give on countless Sundays standing over the podium. Before vanishing into the hall, he patted Mr. Douglas on the shoulder and then closed the door behind him.

What I saw there I've forgotten but replayed in my head a thousand times over. Lily sat on her bed, still and calm with a practiced indifference. The hollow eyes sunken into Mr. Douglas' face were steadfast in their gaze—a predator marking its not so reluctant prey. He took off his jacket and calmly set it on Lily's dresser. Unbuttoning the buttons on his suit vest, his eyes never left her. Inching closer to the bed, he un-tucked his white, button down shirt. As if on cue, when he undid the clasp of his slacks, Lily moved to the head of the bed and lied flat on her back. I'm not sure if I hated Mr. Douglas or her more at that moment but the sight of him unzipping his slacks was too much to bear. I turned away to look at the back of Lily's closet.

What followed was a series of low-toned grunts and emotionless moans. I couldn't say whether it lasted for a minute or an hour, all time had ceased to tick by. Unable to move or breathe, I imagined that's what hell must be like: An eternity of fear, angst, hate, torture and a general inability to do anything about it. I realized I needed to add my name to the list of people I hated in that room.

When the bed stopped squeaking, I waited a minute before I dared to face the door. Mr. Douglas was nonchalantly redressing himself. Once again adorning his slick brown suit, he walked to the door, opened it and left the room without so much as glancing back. Lily lay on her bed, naked, with her back turned to the closet so I couldn't see her face. I thought I heard faint sobs but in the dead silence of the room, I couldn't be sure.

As I was gathering the nerve to emerge from my hiding place there was a knock at the door and, without waiting for an answer, the door was cracked open a few inches.

"Lily," her father's voice came into the room like the calm before a storm. "Your mother and I are going to the supermarket to get something for dinner. We'll be back soon." He waited a moment, and when he got no response he added, "Love you."

Waiting another minute or two, when I was sure Lily's parents had left, I slowly opened the closet door and eased my way out. Lily still had her back to the closet. If she heard me, her body made no mention of it. My brain and vocal chords frozen, all I could do was inch myself closer and closer to the door.

"It was supposed to be you today." Her voice struck from behind me as I opened the door. I turned to look at her one last time. Her vacant, blue eyes only stared at the floor beside her bed. I had something to say on the tip of my tongue—I wanted to call her a whore, to say that I was sorry, to tell her that one day everything would be better—but I understood that, at the moment, no words could possibly matter. The word "today" rang in my head as I descended the stairs and ran out of the front door.

α

The following Sunday was a gauntlet of confusion and guilt. I had barely spoken to anyone in a week and I had avoided Sarah completely. I had a secret and she had a way of relieving my promises to keep secrets, even though I had only promised this one to myself.

And here we all were, once again, sitting in those pews lying to ourselves, being lied to. We were in our usual places: Me with my parents in the second pew from the front, Lily sitting in one of the middle rows with her Sunday School friends and Sarah sitting alone in the back because she refused to sit with her father on the principle that he made her be there. Turning my head slightly to try and steal a glimpse of her from the corner of my eye, I caught her glare. It was strong, unwavering and had a ferocity reserved for those who had been betrayed. Turning back around, my head dropped under the weight of my conscience.

I had tried to play sick that day—I didn't think I could face the sight of Lily's beaming Sunday smile or Mr. Douglas' silent prayer. But my father, the man of stout faith that he was, said that if I wasn't stumbling over myself and vomiting everywhere that I was feeling fine enough to go to church. Mother silently concurred. My hands began trembling while I was getting dressed and even now, holding the hymn book singing "Old Rugged Cross" with a barely audible voice, they had yet to stop.

When Reverend McDermott took his place at the podium to begin the sermon—with his slicked back hair, assuring smile and trustworthy eyes—I felt the blood slowly drain from my face and work its way down my body all the way into my hands, which were already in fists. My appearance must have betrayed me because my mother bent down and quietly asked I was all right.

"I'm fine." I whispered back without looking at her and closed my eyes to try to regain some composure.

Preaching, with the benevolence and conviction he always had, Reverend McDermott had evil on his mind. That day his words warned us of how Lucifer (The carrier of the light, as that is the true meaning of his name) was always around us, tempting us and tricking us.

"From the first book of Peter," he said with one hand holding the Bible and the other up in the air for emphasis, "chapter five, verses eight and nine: *'Be sober-minded; be watchful. Your adversary the devil prowls around like a roaring lion, seeking someone to devour. Resist him, firm in your faith, knowing that the same kinds of suffering are being experienced by your brotherhood throughout the world.'"*

Reverend McDermott continued talking but I could no longer hear him. With his hand still in the air, striking down when he was making a point, all sound had ceased to reach my ears. Perhaps the verses had stricken me deaf or maybe I had finally found a way to shut out the bullshit. Whatever it was, it didn't last long.

"It is no doubt that our world is in peril, my friends," by this time he's walking around the platform in his heated, point-making pacing that he did, "because evil lurks from the shadows and hides in the light. *'And no wonder! For Satan transforms himself into an angel of the light.'* Second Corinthian, chapter eleven, verse fourteen."

I'm not sure if it was the way the sun flowed through the maze of the stained-glass window or if it was just a trick of my mind, but as he stood there rambling—holding the Bible high in the air—the light lied down behind him. Almost seemingly engulfing his essence and illuminating his silhouette against the wall behind him. He was glowing. I craned my neck both ways to see if anyone else saw what I did. They all had their heads staring straight ahead, unmoving, void of emotion with everyone waiting for the next chance to scream hallelujah.

"But don't worry, my friends," he was calming himself down as he always did. He walked back to the podium and eased the Bible back down to its place before him. "Because even though evil exists, God has everything under control." A plethora of "hallelujahs" erupted from the congregation, as if set on a timer. "God tells us through Isaiah: *'I form the light and create darkness: I make peace and create evil: I, the Lord, do all these things.'* Chapter forty-five, verse seven."

The light around him was becoming too much for my eyes to take. Looking away, I turned my head to my right and saw my mother. Sitting here with me and my father, smiling and nodding her head, not showing her concern. Even though she had been in remission for over five years, signs of her cancer were starting to return. Turning my head to my left, I viewed

Lily from the corner of my eyes: Beaming bright with her smile, unaware of her vanished innocence and betrayed love. I didn't even have to look back at Sarah to see her face. She was the only one that could see what I saw. This was evil, and if God was in control of all of this, I wouldn't let Him be in control of me.

"Mother," I whispered. She turned to me after taking a mental note of what Reverend McDermott was saying. Her dark brown eyes bore into me with understanding. I hoped that she would always see me this way. "I'm sorry."

Her eyes followed me as I got up and began to walk down the aisle. After a second, everyone began to look at me. I could feel all of their wonderment weighing me down, but I wouldn't stop walking. Even Reverend McDermott trailed off slightly in his sermon as I imagined him watching me walk away from what he was saying but then he quickly resumed as to not give any merit to my actions.

Eyes locked on one another, I approached Sarah sitting alone in the back pew. I stopped in front of her and offered my hand. With a sense of understanding that went way beyond the words I could've used would have ever went, she took my hand and I helped her up. Hand in hand, with everyone's eyes on us, we opened the doors and walked into the sunlight, leaving the town behind us.

α

I never told anyone about what had happened that day at the McDermott's house. Nobody besides Sarah would've believed me anyway and I didn't want the knowledge burdening her, burrowing a hole into her conscience, like it did mine. Sometimes, when I was bored and Sarah was busy,

I would borrow my Mother's station wagon on the pretense that I just needed to drive around to get some air. Even though I tried to avoid it, on these trips, I would always end up on Birch Court, a few houses down from Lily's, just staring at it. It was like a ghost house. Lily and Matthew never played outside and almost no noise was emitted from the interior. The only use the perfectly trimmed lawn got was when people came or went.

It was a Sunday, a week before the Temple burnt down, and I found myself once again staring at the McDermott's house. I arrived there before the service had ended for the afternoon and had been sitting there for quite some time. The only thing that had happened was that the McDermott's had come home. Just before I turned the ignition to start the car to leave, another car pulled into the driveway. Unable to move, I just stared wide-eyed at the mid-90's model Chevy Blazer that I had seen constantly since I was a child. The engine shut off with a thud from the engine that I had heard so many times. Sarah's father emerged from the vehicle, put his keys in his pocket and whistled to himself, as he often did, while he walked to the front door. The Reverend opened the door a few seconds after the bell was rung. The two men shook hands and seemed to exchange pleasantries for a minute and then Reverend McDermott smiled and nodded his head towards the upstairs. They walked inside and closed the door. I turned the ignition and drove away, my heart ablaze with hatred and adrift in a sea of uncertainty.

α

Walking to the stone wall, dusk was settling over the sky with an eerie hue and an odd scent crawling on the wind.

"Why are we going up here so late?" Sarah asked from a few paces behind me.

"There's something you need to see." I replied with calm that I had never felt before in my life.

"There's never anything new to look at in this town," her voice contained a whining hint that I let go because I knew that she was still in a sour mood from the day before. "And the walk back is gonna be a bitch in the dark, you know that, right?" I smiled to myself in the rays of the faltering sun.

Standing on the stone wall, there was a strange brightness to the dimming sky. When Sarah first saw the flames rising to the horizon from the temple's steeple, she gasped and stood with her lips slightly apart.

"It's beautiful," was all that she said. She put her hand over her heart and I watched the reflection of the fire dance in her eyes and, and in that instant, I saw happiness replace the sadness that had resided there for so long.

I removed the backpack I was carrying, opened it slowly and then emptied its contents onto the ground in front of us. In the fading light given off by the fire the bold white letters could still be made out against the aged, green sign: TEMPLE HILL RD. I watched Sarah stare at the sign and smile as tears crept from her eyes.

Watching the structure begin to give way to the heat, I noticed that the only thing not on fire were the large, white letters that had been planted in the ground at the edge of the plateau for the whole town to see every day: "*Where there is no vision, all shall perish.*" Proverbs, Chapter twenty-nine, verse eighteen.

"I did this for you," I whispered to Sarah.

Turning to look at me, she tried to speak but said nothing. I believe she truly began to understand my gift when she listened and heard no wails of the town's fire trucks, ambulances or police cars. There were no worried cries in the wind of people outside of the temple trying to rescue anyone or put out the fire. She resumed staring at the burning building and slipped her hand into mine. We stood there, hand in hand, staring at the future I had created.

Lightning Source UK Ltd.
Milton Keynes UK
08 February 2011

167130UK00001B/149/P